KU-347-272

'I'm sorry about that... A bit of an overreaction after a tough afternoon. I just hated to see you upset and—well, I...I just wanted to thank you for your help, show you how grateful I am. I didn't mean to overstep the mark!'

Atholl smiled at her. 'But we worked so well together, didn't we? It's just great to know that we have a good working relationship.'

A good working relationship? It had seemed to Terry for a moment there that it had gone beyond a 'working relationship', but she'd obviously misinterpreted it—Atholl was making it very clear that that was what he wanted! It had been nothing more than an over-enthusiastic hug to comfort her.

'It was just part of my job—as you said, a team effort,' she said lightly, and chuckled—as if being kissed by the most stunning-looking man she'd been near for some time was just a normal occurrence, the usual way one thanked a colleague and of no consequence whatsoever...

Judy Campbell is from Cheshire. As a teenager she spent a great year at high school in Oregon, USA, as an exchange student. She has worked in a variety of jobs, including teaching young children, being a secretary and running a small family business. Her husband comes from a medical family, and one of their three grown-up children is a GP. Any spare time—when she's not writing romantic fiction—is spent playing golf, especially in the Highlands of Scotland.

HIRED:
GP AND WIFE

BY
JUDY CAMPBELL

MILLS & BOON®

Pure reading pleasure™

First published in Great Britain 2009
Harlequin Mills & Boon Limited,
Eton House, 18-24 Paradise Road, Richmond, Surrey TW9 1SR

ISBN: 978 0 263 20936 5

Set in Times Roman 10½ on 13 pt
15-0709-51954

Printed and bound in Great Britain
by CPI Antony Rowe, Chippenham, Wiltshire

HIRED:
GP AND WIFE

To Grace, Megan, Louis, George and Joseph
With Love

CHAPTER ONE

THE little ferry edged towards the dock and the deckhand expertly threw the rope round the bollard and tightened it. The gangway slapped down between the land and the boat and everyone began to disembark. Terry Younger stopped for a second and looked around the little bay with the seagulls mewing above the brightly painted cottages across the road and their backdrop of wooded hills.

She took a deep breath of the tangy fresh air and it hit her throat like champagne, invigorating and bracing. The cool wind whipped her short fair hair across her eyes and she brushed it away impatiently, and stepped ashore. Then, hoisting her rucksack more securely on her back, she tugged her case behind her over the rough terrain, a frisson of excitement mixed with apprehension shivering through her for a second. She stopped and looked across the quayside: steep hills rose quickly behind the little village of shops and cottages fringing the bay and beyond them the vague purple outline of mountains. The Isle of Scuola on the west coast of Scotland couldn't be more different to the leafy suburbs of London that she'd left behind—this was it, then, a fresh start, a future that was hers to make of what she would, and find a measure of the peace she craved after the turmoil of a terrible year.

Dumping her baggage by the wall of the dock, Terry looked around at the small group of people waiting to meet the passengers from the ferry. She'd been informed that her new colleague, Dr Brodie, senior partner in the Scuola medical practice, would be picking her up—according to the woman in the medical agency, he was a large, elderly man with white hair. There didn't seem to be anyone of that description here yet—he must be running late, but, no matter, she would sit on her case until he arrived.

After five minutes the ferry had turned round and begun to chug back to the mainland and there was no one left by the quayside except a man in biking leathers sitting astride a motorbike and talking on a mobile. Terry stood up impatiently— she liked to be punctual herself and the later Dr Brodie was the more nervous she was becoming about her new job.

Another ten minutes went by and the man who'd been on the bike was now pacing irritably up and down the quay and looking at his watch. His leathers gave him a tough streetwise appearance and emphasised his tall muscular figure as he strode impatiently in front of Terry. For a second she was cruelly reminded of Max—damn his memory. Wasn't there a hint in the appearance of this man on the quayside of the bad-boy image Max had liked to project? She shut her eyes as if trying to block out a picture of Max swaggering towards her—sexy, arrogant, sure of her love and supremely selfish. She shuddered—she wanted nothing more to do with that sort of man. She snapped open her eyes again and set her mouth grimly. She hadn't come to Scuola to remember him or anything that had happened to her because of him…she had to push all that to the back of her mind.

The biker stopped for a moment in front of her to pull off his helmet, revealing ruffled dark hair, and gazed dourly back at the mainland. Terry flicked a closer look at him—he was quite a striking man, and someone with rather a short fuse, she guessed, full of pent-up energy. As he turned to resume his frustrated pacing, a pen dropped out of his pocket and Terry bent down to pick it up.

'We both seem to have been left in the lurch,' she said, handing it to him.

He turned, looking at her with startling blue eyes, as blue as sapphires, Terry thought suddenly—and of course she realised that he was nothing like Max at all. Max's eyes, although sexy, had often been calculating, as if assessing just what he could gain from you. This man's face had an engaging, open look. His eyes swept over her, taking in her petite figure and resting for an intense moment on her face. The hairs on the back of her neck prickled with a sudden flash of self-consciousness under his scrutiny.

'Ah, thank you,' he said, taking the pen from her, then he added brusquely, 'I think the person I'm meeting must be on the next ferry—if he isn't on this one I'll have to go. Damn nuisance but I can't wait.' He had an attractive voice, fairly deep and with a definite Scottish lilt. He leant against a stone wall that jutted out onto the jetty, long legs crossed in front of him. 'You've been stood up too?' he enquired.

His thick dark hair was a little too long at the front and flopped over onto his forehead—it made him look rather boyish, but there was something tough and determined in his demeanour. He wouldn't suffer fools gladly, thought Terry. She smiled to herself. When it came to men, she couldn't trust herself to interpret character through appearances—her track record was pretty poor on that!

'The man meeting me has either forgotten or had an accident,' she said. 'I'd better get a taxi.'

'Maybe he thinks you'll be on the next ferry too and is coming to meet this one—I can see it in the distance now,' suggested the biker. He pushed himself away from the wall and went to the water's edge, staring across the bay at the approaching vessel.

Terry wondered if he was a tourist who'd come to the island for the fishing or walking. She could well imagine him striding over the hill paths, getting rid of some of his angst with exercise, or roaring over the mountain roads on his motorbike.

They both watched the ferry draw up and disgorge its next lot of passengers, but it was soon apparent that the man's friend had not appeared, and there was still no sign of Dr Brodie. The two of them waited as the three cars on the ferry made their way slowly after the foot passengers down the ramp to shore. The last one was a small two-door car, which stalled and then rolled back onto the ship, and the driver, a young woman, looked anxiously out of the window.

'Give it more stick, miss,' advised the deckhand in charge of the vehicles. 'You need to accelerate to get over the humps on the ramp.'

The girl nodded and tried again, revving the engine hard, and this time the car shot forward and skidded over the ramp. It took half a second for Terry to realise with horror that it was arrowing straight across the space between them like a missile fixed on a target. Her feet seemed to be paralysed, be stuck in thick clay—she could see the car careering for them but she couldn't move her body or even cry out. Then, at the last moment when the car seemed almost on top of her, two arms flung themselves tightly round her and she felt herself being lifted away from the danger and dropped not too gently on the ground, underneath her rescuer.

For a second she was winded—unable to breathe or speak—but she was aware that in the background there was the nasty sound of a heavy crash, metal being crushed and breaking glass, then a shocked silence. The body on top of hers scrambled off, allowing her to see the car embedded in the wall of the dock.

'Bloody hell,' said a voice over her head. 'That was a bit too close for comfort!'

She blinked in a dazed way, and found herself gazing into the intensely bright blue eyes she'd just been looking at a few minutes before.

'You OK?' asked the biker. A large graze covered with grit on his chin oozed blood and his thick hair was plastered on his forehead. 'Here, let me help you up.'

'Yes…yes, I'm fine,' she replied, using the strong grip of his hand to get up slowly and shakily to her feet. Her trousers and parka were covered with dirt, but she was alive—thanks to the man.

He looked at her closely then nodded. 'Good. Then I'll see what's happened to the driver.'

Terry watched, stunned, as he sprinted over to the car and peered through the driver's window then tried to pull open the door. She couldn't believe how rapid his reactions had been as the car had hurtled towards them, or how quickly he'd re-covered himself to think of the other people involved.

She scrambled up from the ground herself and ran after him to the car, where he was already trying to force the driver's door open. It was a horrific sight, the front stoved in and as crumpled as a piece of crushed foil. The girl in the driving seat turned towards them, looking utterly shocked. An egg-shaped bruise on her forehead was rapidly enlarging and a gash above her eye was pouring blood. She put a shaking hand up to her forehead and started to whimper.

'Wh-what happened there? I…I just touched the accelerator and it took off…'

The biker pushed his hand through the door and turned off the ignition. 'Sometimes these automatic gear changes are quite fierce,' he said gently. He tilted her chin towards the light and examined her forehead as he talked to her. 'What's your name?'

'Maisie…Maisie Lockart,' the girl whispered. Then her eyes widened as she remembered something and she started to scream, trying to turn round in the seat to look at the back. 'Oh, my God…the baby…Amy…she's in the back. Is she all right? Get her out please…get her out!'

Terry looked aghast at the concertinaed front of the car and the way the passenger seat was pushed back right against the rear. There wasn't going to be much room for even a child sitting in the back. She heard the man swear as he gave a desperate tug on the driver's door again and managed to open it another precious half-foot. He peered in the back then gave a little whoop of relief.

'Yes! She's OK. You won't believe this, but she appears to be smiling at me!' He pulled back and said gently to the girl, 'Don't worry—she looks fine, kicking her legs. From here everything looks in working order.'

The girl closed her eyes and put her head back against the back of the seat. 'Thank God,' she whispered. 'Can you get hold of her?'

Terry tapped the man's back. 'Perhaps I could help?' she said. 'I'm a doctor.'

The biker whipped his head round and looked at her with raised brows of surprise. 'Well, well, that's a bit of a coincidence—I'm a doctor too! I must say it's nice to have some support.' He turned back to the girl in the car and commented with gentle humour, 'Funny, isn't it? You can wait all day for a doctor and then two come along at once!'

The girl gave a watery smile. 'We're in good hands, then, aren't we?'

The man turned to Terry and said in a low voice, 'As you can see, she's had a terrific crack to her head and I wouldn't be surprised if she's not got a whiplash injury to her neck. I think you'll agree she needs a check-up and an X-ray. I'll ring for an ambulance if you take over here for a second. Better not to move her at this stage.'

'What about the baby?' said Terry, peering into the back of the vehicle. 'We can't leave her on the back seat. On the other hand, I agree it's risky to move Maisie. We could disturb a fractured vertebrae or a subluxation.'

'Yep. We've got to be cautious if she's displaced a joint,' he agreed.

For a second they looked at each other, trying to weigh up the pros and cons of the problem, then Terry said with decision, 'The little one does seem reasonably happy. I'll watch them and try and stop this bleed above Maisie's eye while you get help.'

'OK. It should only be a matter of minutes…'

Terry scrabbled in her rucksack until she found a packet of tissues, which she pressed firmly against the wound. Maisie had started to shake and tears rolled down her cheeks.

'I'm sorry… I don't mean to make a fuss, but I can't go to hospital—I've got papers to deliver. And what about the baby?'

Terry laid her hand reassuringly over Maisie's, recognising the signs of shock in the girl. 'Don't worry about the papers—they'll get sorted. Just tell me the baby's name.'

'Amy—she's only four months. And…and she'll need a bottle soon.'

'Look, Maisie, you both must go and be checked over and however well Amy looks it's best to make sure she has no hidden injury. They'll want to observe her for a few hours and if she needs feeding, the hospital will make sure she's looked after. And I'll see the papers are delivered if you'll tell me where they're to go to.'

'Thank you,' whispered the girl. 'They go to the newsagent's, Mathesons, just across the road from here.' She sighed bleakly, 'I don't know how I'll tell my boyfriend. It's his car and he'll be furious I've crashed it.'

'He'll just be glad you're both OK,' reassured Terry.

Terry's eyes followed the doctor pacing about the car park as he spoke on his mobile. She might have guessed he'd be a doctor, a policeman or a fireman—someone who was used to dealing with emergencies. He had the confidence of knowing what he was doing, and it showed—he was someone you could trust, she thought wistfully. Then she shrugged irritably, cross with herself for thinking that. Just because he was a doctor, it didn't mean he'd be any more reliable than anyone else. Didn't she know only too well that even the most credible of people could let you down and ruin your life?

The biker doctor came back, stuffing his mobile in his pocket.

'It'll be here very soon…' He halted, his expression

suddenly changing to one of alarm as he sniffed the air. 'Hell! We've got to get them out, pronto,' he yelled. 'Can't you smell the petrol? There must be a leak. The damn thing could go up in flames any second. Let me undo that safety belt.'

He turned to the small crowd of onlookers gathered a short distance from them. 'We need a man here to help us,' he shouted.

Two or three men ran forward. 'Tell us what you want us to do,' said one of them.

'Help me slide Maisie out and lift her carefully, supporting her neck, and if two others could take her legs. Then we need to get that baby out of the back.'

For a moment Terry felt herself back in Casualty, forming part of a team in an emergency where split-second decisions had to be taken. This man was right, of course. The risk of fire was imminent, and they had no choice but to get the people out as quickly as possible. She helped to hold Maisie's back as they edged her out, her neck being supported by the doctor, who shouted out instructions to the others, then they laid her on Terry's jacket which she'd put on the ground.

Terry squeezed Maisie's hand comfortingly. It was vital that the girl, already in shock, was kept as calm as possible. 'Now it's Amy's turn,' she said.

The aperture to the back of the car was very small, constrained by the buckling of the car's chassis. No way could a large man get through it.

'I'm doing this,' said Terry firmly. 'I can get through that space.'

'Oh, no, you won't.' The biker tried to push in front of her. 'It's up to me—it's too damn dangerous.'

'And you're too damn big to get through,' retorted Terry angrily. 'I thought you said there's no time to waste. Don't let's argue about it.'

Their eyes sparked across at each other aggressively for a second then reluctantly he gave way, allowing her to push herself into the small opening.

'You win,' he muttered. 'I'll try and force this door a bit more.'

By squeezing herself sideways, she managed to wriggle her body to the squashed rear of the car. Stretching forward with every sinew, she reached the baby and fumbled with the child's safety harness. It seemed terribly difficult to undo but behind her she could hear the distinctive deep voice of the biker.

'You're doing well. Press the button in the middle of the harness firmly and squeeze the two sides together…sometimes they're quite stiff.'

There was something reassuring about that measured voice and when Amy began to scream as this unfamiliar person tried to extricate her from her seat, Terry concentrated on what the biker was telling her and did her best to ignore the smell of petrol that seemed to get stronger every second.

'It's all right, darling—don't cry. You'll soon be with your mummy,' she murmured in her most soothing tones whilst still struggling desperately with the catch on the harness. Suddenly the spring release worked and the belt came apart.

'Ah…gotcha!' she said triumphantly.

She pulled the child towards her, hugging her to her chest and backing out as quickly as she could. Waiting hands took the crying baby to the side of the car park near to where her mother was lying, and Terry toppled back as someone's arms caught her and prevented her falling to the ground.

'Well done,' said the biker's familiar voice gruffly. 'You did a good job there.' His arms held her close to him as he helped her across to the side of the car park. 'Come on, now—let's get you away from this vehicle.'

Her legs felt like jelly but he took her weight easily, almost carrying her to one of the benches by the dock railings. He took off his leather jacket and put it round Terry's shoulders and she gave a shaky laugh. 'You seem to make a habit of helping me.'

He leaned forward and brushed away a piece of mud that was on her cheek. 'Sure you're OK?' he asked, smiling at her, his face so close to hers that she could see the beginnings of evening stubble on his chin and the dark flecks in his extraordinarily blue eyes.

His breath was on her cheek as he looked at her and unexpectedly she felt a funny little shock of attraction ripple through her body. She took a sharp intake of breath and got up hastily from the bench, stepping back from him unsteadily. What the hell was happening? Not so long ago her life had been ruined by a man and she'd vowed it would be a long time before she'd look at the opposite sex again. Here she was only fifteen minutes into her new life and behaving like a schoolgirl who'd just seen a pop star! Her goal when she came to Scuola was to devote her life to medicine and put romance behind her—and that was what she was going to do!

'I...I'm perfectly fine,' she said in a measured tone.

His eyes held hers for a second, his expression contrite. 'I'm afraid I was a bit abrupt with you back then. I just didn't want you putting yourself in danger.'

'We both had cross words—all in the line of duty,' she replied. Quickly she went to kneel beside Maisie and her baby, who was in the arms of one of the men who had been helping, and pushed this hunky guy to the back of her thoughts.

'You'll soon be in good hands,' she comforted the young girl. 'And little Amy looks very lively.'

'Thank you,' whispered Maisie. 'Thank you for getting Amy out. I thought she'd be trapped.'

A few minutes later a police car sped into the car park, followed by an old-fashioned ambulance.

'That car reeks of petrol,' the biker doctor said to the officer who got out of the car. 'I've turned off the ignition, but I'm frightened it might ignite.'

Without a word the officer pulled a fire extinguisher out of his car and started to douse the back of the crashed vehicle with foam, then he shouted to the onlookers, 'Can you clear this area please? This car's not safe to be near and we need room for the ambulance.'

Two paramedics jumped out of the ambulance, one with a medical bag, and the doctor went up to them and explained in his concise and brisk manner the circumstances of the accident. Terry kept up a comforting commentary to Maisie until they came over, noting how she had begun to relax slightly now she was out of the vehicle and her baby was safe.

The paramedics swiftly assessed Maisie's condition, then put a brace round her neck and lifted her onto a board to support her back before placing her on a carrying stretcher. Then she was put in the ambulance with Amy, and Terry and the biker watched as it disappeared up the hill.

Terry sat down on the bench and leaned back, closing her eyes, a mixture of relief and tiredness flooding through her.

The doctor chuckled. 'What you need is a wee dram—that'll put new life in you!'

She opened her eyes to see the doctor bending down beside her, a grin on his mud-bespattered face, blood still oozing from his chin.

Terry shook her head and smiled. 'I'm fine, thanks. In fact, it's quite exhilarating when you get a good result after a bit of drama.' She felt in the front pocket of her knapsack and pulled out a compact, grimacing at her reflection in the mirror. 'What a wreck I look,' she murmured to herself.

'Just a bit mud-spattered,' he said. 'Nothing a good wash won't remove!'

Terry watched as the man picked up his helmet and searched in his pockets for the key to his bike. She realised just what she owed to this stranger, and reflected that her little flicker of attraction to him a few seconds before was probably because of the emotional rebound that often happened after a traumatic event.

'I have such a lot to thank you for. If you hadn't had such lightning reactions I wouldn't be here now,' she said to him. 'I was paralysed when I saw the car coming towards me—I couldn't move. You saved my life, no doubt.'

'Think nothing of it. You didn't do so badly yourself, getting that baby out. The whole thing could have gone up in flames any second.'

Terry shivered. 'It was the same for you getting Maisie out—a nightmare scenario,' she murmured. She looked at the cut on his chin. 'You know, you ought to have that graze cleaned—it's quite deep and got a lot of dirt in it.'

'Oh, I'll see to it when I get back,' he said carelessly, then looked at her with interest. 'Is this your first visit to Scuola?'

'Yes…not quite the start I wanted,' admitted Terry. She glanced at the smashed car. 'I did promise Maisie that I'd get the papers in her car delivered to that newsagent's over the road.'

'No problem. I'll do that afterwards.'

'Thank you.' She started to take off the leather jacket he'd put over her in the car park. 'You'd better have this back.'

He looked at his watch. 'No, you hang onto it for a while, it's getting very cold. Perhaps I could give you a lift now,' he offered. 'I can't hang around here any longer and it seems as if your chap's forgotten to come and mine must have missed some connection.'

Terry looked nervously at the large machine he was proposing to give her a lift on—not her favourite form of transport. 'Er…that's very kind of you. The trouble is, I've got no helmet.'

Amused eyes twinkled at her as if he guessed her anxiety. 'Don't worry—I bought a spare with me. Where are you going?'

'Not very far. A place called The Sycamores—it's the medical centre on the island, and I believe it's off the main street.'

The man straightened up suddenly from getting out the spare helmet from the bike's holdall and stared at her in surprise. 'You're going to the medical centre?'

'I'm going to start a new job there,' explained Terry simply.

The man pushed his fingers through his hair so that it stood up in ruffled spikes round his forehead. 'So you're not on holiday, then? I thought you were a tourist.'

Terry shook her head. 'Far from it.'

'Who were you expecting to meet you?' he said slowly.

'Dr Euan Brodie. Do you know him?'

He gave a short laugh. 'I ought to—he's my uncle. I'm Atholl Brodie and I've come to meet a Terry Younger who's taking over from a locum at our practice. Unfortunately my uncle had a major heart attack three days ago and is in hospital on the mainland. I'm sorry I didn't get round to telling the agency that it would be me meeting you and not Uncle Euan. I'm his partner in the practice.'

Terry felt a funny thrill of excitement—could this really be the guy she was going to work with? 'We…we've found each other, then. I'm Terry Younger.' She held out her hand and he shook it rather abstractedly.

'So I gather,' he replied with a wry smile. 'I have to admit this is, er…rather a surprise.'

'Oh? Why is that?'

'Because I thought you'd be a man,' he said simply. 'It didn't occur to me that Terry could be a girl's name as well.'

'Well, I hope it's not too much of a let-down,' Terry said.

'No…no, of course not. But do you know that on top of GP duties to cover the two islands here, we at the practice help a friend of mine doing an outward bound course for four deprived teenagers from Glasgow for a few weeks? I was hoping that the new doctor—'

'Would be six foot four and sixteen stone,' finished Terry impishly. 'As a matter of fact, I did know your requirements,' she added, smiling. 'The agency told me you wanted help with the course.'

Atholl's eyes swept over her slight five-foot-four-inch frame and he shook his head dismissively. 'These lads are large, rough and aggressive. I need someone who's physically tough and can abseil down cliffs, lead hikes on mountain trails, keep discipline—ideally someone who's had a course in Outward Bound activities…'

'And why shouldn't I be able to fulfil all those criteria?' demanded Terry. Suddenly his looks seemed to diminish—

he was a more unreasonable man than she'd thought, obviously dismissing females as pathetic creatures who couldn't do anything physically demanding.

She added firmly, 'It so happens I have done a three-day course in hiking and kayaking—the only thing I've not done is abseiling. Anyway, if you think I'm getting back on that ferry today you've got another think coming. I've been offered a job here and I've accepted it, and it's taken since the crack of dawn to get here.'

A cold wind had blown up suddenly and a stinging rain was starting to drive in from the hills. Terry pulled the helmet over her head and stared at him stubbornly. The man may have just saved her life, but she was damned if she'd go meekly trotting back to London just because he'd been expecting a man. Not, she thought wanly, that returning would be an option anyway—she could never return to London.

Atholl shrugged and then picked up Terry's case and rucksack.

'I guess we'll sort it all out later,' he said. 'We'll leave your case at the ferry office and I'll come back for it shortly, after we've talked at the surgery.' He looked down at her with a sudden laugh that made his strong face look younger, softer. 'And I thought Terry was a man's name…is it short for something?'

'No,' said Terry with deliberate emphasis. 'It's just Terry.'

She clambered on the back of his motorbike, and bit her lip. It wasn't just her name—that was who she'd become now, Terry Younger, looking different and feeling different from a few days ago, cut off from the family and friends of her old life, with a whole new persona.

She was on her own, and it was vitally important to her that her job worked out here. She was as far away from London as she could reasonably get and still be in the British Isles—she wasn't about to go anywhere else in a hurry.

CHAPTER TWO

'PUT your arms round me,' shouted Atholl through the wind, 'and lean with the bike!'

He was one powerfully built man—muscles like steel bars, thought Terry as she clung to him nervously, wrapping her arms round him like a vice. She gave a surprised giggle. What girl wouldn't choose to be in her situation? Hugging a man who looked as if he did a daily workout in the gym as close to her body as she could!

Then she closed her eyes in fright as he roared along the winding road out of the little bay and up the hill beyond the colourful cottages on the seafront, the bike leaning frighteningly at an angle when they turned corners. There was probably no need to worry about the job, she decided resignedly. She'd be killed on this bike before she got to the surgery.

They pulled up sharply in the drive of a gracious-looking stone-built house covered with scaffolding. Terry dismounted carefully, wondering if Atholl had deliberately driven the blessed machine at the speed of light to test her nerve or if it just seemed that way.

'You OK?' he asked.

'Of course. I found it exhilarating,' Terry retorted as she

removed her helmet. She was damned if she'd let him believe she was a wimp!

She turned to look around at the view—or as much as she could see in the driving rain. It was spectacular, dramatic and gloomy with black clouds looming over the Sound of Scuola. The mainland over the water was just a dark line on the horizon at the moment.

'When the sky's clear and there's sunshine it's a completely different picture—the sea is as blue as a periwinkle. And believe me,' he added with a grin, 'it does stop raining sometimes! Now, come in and get dry and perhaps we can discuss arrangements over coffee and some biscuits.'

It was warm inside—the large hall did duty as a waiting room, and another room with half the wall cut out formed the reception area, with a severe-looking grey-haired woman behind the desk. She looked up as they came in.

'You've taken your time, Atholl,' she remarked sternly. 'You've several calls to do before we finish tonight.' She peered at his face. 'And what have you done to your chin— fallen off your bike? I told you that machine was lethal…and your uncle hates you riding it.'

'Nothing to do with the bike—just a fall, Isobel,' he said lightly.

'And what about this Dr Younger—where is he? You said you were going to meet him.'

He put his hand behind Terry's shoulder and drew her forward, saying drily, 'This is Dr Younger—she just travelled up from London today. Terry, this is Isobel Nash, one of our receptionists.'

Isobel stared back at Terry with surprise, taking in her bedraggled appearance wearing a leather jacket several sizes too big for her, and said bluntly, 'But she's a woman. We thought from the name that they were sending a man.'

Terry sighed and looked from Atholl to Isobel. There seemed to be a general prejudice against females here!

Atholl saw her expression and explained, 'Apart from having to deal with the teenage lads I told you about, I thought a man might fit more easily into this job for, er, various reasons.'

His glance flicked across to Isobel, who looked grimmer than ever and pursed her lips, saying, 'It's not only that— where's the poor lass to sleep?'

Terry put down her dripping rucksack. 'Look, I'm sorry I'm not who you both thought I was, but do you mind if I get dry while you discuss this?'

'Ah, yes, of course…' Atholl's expression was faintly embarrassed, as if he realised how rude he'd been. 'Isobel, can you rustle up some tea and biscuits for us? We'll go into my room, Terry, and you can dry out a bit. I'll take the leather jacket.'

Terry followed him feeling slightly deflated, her excitement in coming to the island rather dashed by the mixed welcome she'd received. It had been a long day's journey from London and coupled with the drama at the quayside she felt emotionally drained and now worried that she'd come all this way for nothing. How easy would it be to work with someone who had been expecting to engage a man? She gave an inward shrug. She'd just have to show him that she was as good if not better than anyone else would have been.

She took off the damp cardigan she'd been wearing under the borrowed coat, and handed it to Atholl, who draped it over a radiator. She rubbed her hair with the towel he offered and while she was drying herself he walked over to a filing cabinet, took out a file and started to read it. Terry looked at him covertly through the folds of the towel. He really had the rugged good looks and powerful physique of a man used to the outdoors—and she had reason to be grateful that he was pretty strong, she reflected, strong enough to lift her bodily off the ground with seconds to spare when a car was heading towards them.

She suspected that his brisk manner indicated he was the type of person who liked things done his way and was fairly outspoken when put out about something—like getting a woman as a locum when he expected a man! It was such an old-fashioned attitude, she thought irritably. He was probably married to a little mousy woman who wouldn't say boo to a goose.

Atholl glanced up when he'd perused the file and flicked an assessing eye over her as she finished rubbing her hair dry, running her fingers through her short curls so that they formed a crisp halo round her face. He wasn't at all sure that she was the right sort of person to take on this particular job. He would always be worried about her ability to cope with some of the tearaways that he and Pete had taken on—but even more to the point, and most importantly, his experience with the last locum had convinced him that there were too many pitfalls where women colleagues in a small practice were concerned. Especially, he thought with sudden awareness, when the woman was as attractive as Terry Younger! Not, of course, from his point of view—he was damn well finished with women and relationships for a long, long time—more from the aspect of his patients and friends who were all longing to fix him up with the next single woman who came into his orbit.

He sighed and sat down in the chair, leaning forward with his elbows on the desk. If they were going to work together, he ought to find out more about her.

'So you've come up from London today—that's quite a long journey.'

'That's right. I started at the crack of dawn. The agency sent all my particulars a few days ago, except obviously to state that I was a woman,' Terry said drily.

He gave a rather abashed smile. 'I've got the file here. I can't have read it properly,' he admitted. 'It does indeed say you're female—I'm afraid I just looked at your name, Terry Younger, and assumed they'd sent me a man.'

'Well, they haven't pulled the wool over your eyes, have they? Anyway, here I am!'

He blinked at her forthright attitude, and his mouth twitched with amusement. 'You are indeed! Sit down for a moment.' He put the file down on the desk and looked at her curiously. 'You've got some excellent references and it seemed you had a good job in London. What made you want to leave?'

Terry had been expecting that question and even though she'd rehearsed her reply many times, she felt her throat constrict and to her ears her voice sounded rushed and breathless.

She swallowed, trying to let the half-lies she was telling seem light and matter-of-fact. 'I…I felt it was time for a change. I've been living in London since I qualified. I love the outdoor life and it's been a dream of mine to work in Scotland in a rural area for a long time.'

'Can't be easy, leaving friends and family in the South… they'll surely miss you,' he remarked, his clear eyes flicking over her searchingly. Her heart began to thump. Did he suspect that there'd been something amiss in her past?

She forced a smile. 'Oh, I've not got much family down there now, although of course I shall miss some things,' she said. 'But it's good to have a change, and I like the idea of being in a small community.'

'A small *remote* community. Why choose Scuola—why not the mainland?'

'When the agency mentioned the job and I looked the place up on the internet, it looked so beautiful—such a contrast to London. And remote sounds rather good to me.'

'You didn't want a permanent position?'

'I thought it would be nice to experience a few jobs and get around a bit, having worked in the same place for a some years.' And the fact, she thought bleakly, that she had to resist putting down roots, uneasy that the past might catch up with her some time.

He nodded, seemingly satisfied with this explanation. 'And do you come from a medical family? Are either of your parents doctors?'

She knew the question was casual, a polite enquiry to show that he was interested in her background, but she wasn't prepared for the tight little knot of distress that formed in her throat or the way her cheeks flamed. She'd developed a kind of protective amnesia where her father was concerned but when something jolted her into thinking about him a powerful image of that terrible day when her world had stopped leapt into her mind—and the knowledge that she could never live again in London without the fear of danger always at her shoulder.

'No, my mother was a homemaker until she passed away while I was in my teens. And my father had nothing to do with medicine…nothing at all. He was in the financial world,' she stumbled.

Atholl said very gently, 'Has your father died too?'

Terry nodded and swallowed, pushing back the memories. 'Yes…he had a heart attack a few weeks ago.'

'I'm sorry. It must be a very difficult time for you.'

Difficult enough for her to leave her roots in London, Atholl surmised. He could imagine her background—affluent and comfortable, a girl who probably went to a private school and lived in a pleasant residential area of London. A city girl…just like Zara had been, he reflected bitterly.

He was prevented from asking further questions by the door opening and Isobel coming in bearing a tray with two mugs, a teapot and a plate with some scones, butter and jam on it.

'Here's your tea,' she said brusquely, putting it down on the desk. She looked in her dour way at Terry. 'You're not from these parts, then?'

Terry sighed. It seemed that people wanted to know a lot about her, and she wanted to tell them as little as possible!

'No, I'm not. But it looks a beautiful place—even when it's pouring with rain!'

Isobel's stern face softened slightly and she said, 'Well, I hope you'll be happy.' She looked sternly at Atholl. 'Now, make sure yon lass eats these home-made scones. I've heated them up and she must be starving after coming all that way from London.'

Isobel nodded curtly at them both and then went out to answer the phone that was ringing shrilly in Reception.

'I suspect Isobel's bark is worse than her bite,' remarked Terry.

Atholl chuckled. 'She's as soft as butter inside, but she's bullied and bossed Uncle Euan around for thirty years now— she thinks she runs the practice.'

'And is your uncle very ill?'

'He's making good progress.' Atholl sighed. 'The truth is I think he'll retire now. He was on half-time before, winding down a bit.'

'And that's why you needed someone else to help? Was my predecessor here long?'

A slight tightening of the lips and Atholl's expression changed. 'Not very long,' he replied briefly. He got up from his seat and went over to the table. 'Now, let's have this tea, and perhaps we can sort a few things out.'

He handed her a cup and the plate of scones whose lovely warm smell had been wafting tantalisingly across to Terry. Suddenly she realised how very hungry and thirsty she was— it had been many hours since she'd had anything to eat. She took a huge gulp of the hot strong liquid and its warmth surged comfortingly through her, then she bit into the warm scone covered with melting butter and thickly coated with raspberry jam. No doubt about it, Isobel was a wonderful cook.

He smiled as he watched her face. 'Ready for that, were you?'

'I'm starving,' she admitted. 'I don't care how many calories were in it!'

The blue eyes flicked over her for a second. 'I don't think there's any need for you to worry,' he observed shortly.

She noted his brief comment wryly—it was so different from the flowery response she'd have expected from Max, who had scattered compliments about like confetti—especially when he'd wanted something. How he'd loved to flatter. It made her embarrassed to remember how taken in she'd been by his patronising and glib remarks. But she'd learned her lesson now—she'd never be duped by that kind of gushing sentiment again.

She pushed unwelcome thoughts about Max to the back of her mind and put the plate down. 'Right,' she said crisply. 'You wanted to sort a few things out, so fire away!'

He leaned back and folded his arms. 'Did you mean it when you said you liked the outdoor life? To be frank, you'd be asked to do a lot of things that you wouldn't do in London. To start with there's the mountain rescue team that we are part of. You could be called out day or night, winter or summer— it's not just a hike up the hillside.'

'Tell me what to do and I'll do it.' Terry looked at him challengingly. 'The agency warned me there would be outside duties and I'm prepared for that—it sounds interesting. Anyway, I bet I wouldn't be the only woman on that team. Surely they aren't all men?'

'As a matter of fact they are,' he said. 'And we can't afford to have a weak link in the chain.'

A flash of irritation whipped through her and she sprang up from her chair. 'Look, I wouldn't let you down but, hey, if you can't face working with a woman here please tell me now and I'll take the next ferry back to the mainland and find a job somewhere else. Let's not waste each other's time.'

He looked slightly taken aback at her petite, feisty figure standing rather pugnaciously opposite him, then his face relaxed and he hid a broad grin behind his hand as he stroked his chin reflectively. Terry Younger didn't mind saying what she felt, although he had a gut feeling that there was more to her story about the real reason she'd left London. She'd seemed vaguely uncomfortable when answering some of his questions.

He knew only too well from his own experience that it was often a seismic event in one's life that made one up sticks and move to a another location. But it took guts to come up all this way north without knowing anyone and leaving one's friends behind, and hadn't she just proved she was no slouch in an emergency? Perhaps, he pondered, she wouldn't be such a bad choice after all—and where was he going to get another doctor at short notice, just as the tourist season on Scuola was starting? He couldn't afford to be too choosy, and he'd just have to put up with having a woman to work with, however wary he was after his experience with Zara Grahame, his previous locum.

He twiddled a pencil in his fingers thoughtfully for a second, then, making a sudden decision, stood up abruptly. 'I don't think you'd let anyone down, Terry. After all, I've just had evidence of it half an hour ago at the accident by the dockside. If you think you can hack it here, I'll be pleased to welcome you aboard!'

He held out his hand, his bright blue eyes smiling into hers, and she almost laughed with relief that he sounded quite happy to work with her after all. An extraordinary tremor of excitement and something else she couldn't quite define crackled through her as they shook hands. The thought of working with Atholl Brodie was promising an unknown, perhaps dangerous but exciting flight into the future.

She took a deep breath and grinned at him. 'Thank you, Atholl—and I'll make sure you never have any complaints that I'm not up to the job, even though I'm a woman!'

'I won't ever hold that against you, I promise.' He smiled. 'Have you any questions to ask me?'

'Isobel mentioned something about accommodation difficulties, but the agency said there was a small flat that went with the job?'

'There's a flat in the building,' he admitted. 'But perhaps

you noticed the scaffolding on the side of the house? I'm afraid my uncle let the place go a little, to say the least, and there's a lot of damp and mould. Your flat's not fit to live in at the moment.'

'So where do you suggest I sleep?' asked Terry lightly. 'Perhaps a bed and breakfast?'

'Might be difficult over the next few days—there's a folk festival on this weekend and the place is booked solid. My suggestion is that you come to my place...' He hesitated a moment. 'I'm afraid it's a bit ramshackle and rather basic— we're in the process of doing it up. To be frank, I didn't think it would matter if a man was taking the job, but seeing...'

'I'm a woman?' finished off Terry wryly. 'For goodness' sake, if there's a bed and a shower somewhere in the building I'll be perfectly happy.' She frowned slightly. 'You said "we" are doing it up. I don't want to be any bother to your wife...'

'I was referring to the friend who's running this outward bound course for boys,' Atholl said. 'He's helping me with a bit of building work and decorating—and the boys are involved too, which keeps them busy.'

'So do they all live there as well? It must be rather crowded.'

Atholl laughed. 'Certainly not. I share the house with Shona...she's a darling and keeps an eye on the place when I'm not there. I don't know where I'd be without her.'

'Oh...I see. Are you sure there'll be room, then, and that Shona won't mind?'

His eyes danced. 'Plenty of room, and Shona will be ecstatic, I know.'

Was Shona his girlfriend or some dear old housekeeper? wondered Terry, feeling oddly deflated. Perhaps it was the fact that there would be another person living close to her who would want to know all about her, another person to convince that there was nothing untoward about her coming to Scuola. It would have been nice, she thought wistfully, to have had a place to herself so that she could relax after work and not bother about anyone else or their probing questions into her background. Still, perhaps this arrangement would not last too long.

'I suggest I take you there now,' Atholl said. 'You can have a hot bath and help yourself to whatever you want to eat—at least,' he corrected himself with a grin, 'whatever there might be in the fridge. You must be starving.'

'Won't Shona mind me rooting around in the kitchen?'

'Shona will probably join you in whatever you dig out.' He grinned. 'We'll call in at the harbour master's office for your case—and, don't worry, we'll take the Land Rover this time. Even I don't fancy the thought of balancing a case on the bike.

'I'm taking Terry to the cottage,' he told Isobel as they crossed the hall. 'Forward any calls to me on my mobile. I'll do all my visits after that.'

Isobel nodded rather dourly. 'I hope you've got some food in.'

Atholl looked at his receptionist rather defiantly. 'And you'll be pleased to know that Terry's going to be joining us in the practice.'

Even though I'm a girl, thought Terry wryly.

Isobel pursed her lips. 'I hope it works out…'

Terry looked up at him questioningly as they walked out of the house. 'She sounds very dubious about me working here,' she remarked.

He shrugged. 'She a bit of a pessimist where I'm concerned,' he said enigmatically.

* * *

The weather had changed in the time they'd been inside. The dark clouds had been blown away and now an eggshell-blue sky was spreading from the west and lighting up the tops of the hills with pale sunshine. Suddenly the place looked far less forbidding and the hedges and trees that arched across the road as they drove along had a fresh green newly washed quality about them. Atholl pointed out various landmarks and told Terry more about the practice on the journey.

'You might think that the practice is only big enough for one doctor,' he remarked. 'But we look after two islands here—there's a little ferry that goes over to the smaller island of Hersa. I do a clinic there once a week but, of course, if there's a real emergency we have a helicopter, which is part of the air sea rescue team.'

'It sounds very varied. How do you get around on Hersa?'

He laughed. 'That's where the motorbike comes in useful. I take it with me on the ferry. There are a lot of patients who live in remote places, not just on Hersa but here as well—it's useful when they can't get to see us. And we're just into the tourist season so the population almost doubles.'

'What do the tourists do?'

He laughed. 'Besides fishing, walking, golf and deer stalking? There's two distilleries to visit and the big hotel has tennis courts and a swimming pool. And then there's climbing on the mountains you see over there—a very good source of patients,' he said grimly. 'It's amazing the number of naive people who try to get to the top totally without equipment or experience.'

What a contrast to her patch in London, thought Terry. It was almost too much to take in, and she was gradually becoming aware that it wasn't going to be the sort of quiet country practice she'd imagined.

'I'll need to get some transport,' she said. 'And I'd rather not borrow your motorbike!'

'Don't worry about that—you can use Uncle Euan's little car. The main thing is to take a map and your mobile—it's easy to get lost in the hills out there.'

'It's all very beautiful.' Terry peered through the car window at the changing scene in front of them. 'There must be some wonderful walks—I can't wait to explore.'

Atholl smiled. 'There's so many different walks along the shore and back through the woods and the hills I never tire of them.' He glanced at her and said in an offhand way, 'You'd be welcome to come with a small group of us who walk together sometimes if you like.'

Funny how much that suggestion pleased her—she'd been sad for so long that the slightest lifting of her spirits felt almost alien. It was as if a curtain had been drawn apart a little and a small beam of sunlight had filtered through.

'I'd enjoy that very much,' she said. 'Were you born here?'

He shook his head. 'No, I only came here in the school holidays. I was born and raised in Glasgow.'

'I believe it's a lovely city.'

'I lived in a very deprived area,' he explained. 'There's still a lot of poverty in parts of Glasgow, and my family lived—still do really—in a pretty poor way. Not many advantages to life in the area I was brought up in.'

He'd obviously been glad to leave, thought Terry, whereas she had been so very happy with her life in London until…until it had all crumbled around about her ears and she'd been forced to depart. She sighed and leaned back in her seat, trying to blank out that last vision she'd had of her father as he'd lain dying in her arms and her frantic efforts to save him.

She bit her lip, telling herself firmly that she'd just got to put that episode in her life behind her. All that was finished and done with now.

'So you won't go back to live there, then,' she commented.

He shrugged, a wry smile touching his lips. 'My family think I should be back with them. They think I've let them down—sort of leaving the sinking ship kind of thing and coming to a better area when I could be of much more use where they live.' He gave a humourless laugh. 'They imagine I'm hobnobbing with lairds and big landowners—well above my station in life!'

'That's ridiculous!' cried Terry. 'You're helping your uncle out—and you're needed here as well!'

He laughed at her response. 'Nevertheless, perhaps they have a point. The fact is, though, that I needed to get more experience—have a wider take on life. I'd lived and trained there all my life, and I was longing to spread my wings. And once I'd started working here, I fell in love with the place.'

He changed gear and slowed as they turned a corner and drew up in front of a square stone cottage surrounded by a little copse and protected from the road by a small front garden.

'Here we are—rough and ready perhaps, but it's home to me,' he remarked.

The cottage wasn't very big, but was most attractive, with a Virginia creeper running rampant over the walls and an untidy rose scrambling round the front door. Terry descended from the Land Rover rather wearily and followed Atholl as he went to the front door and opened it.

He whistled as he went into the little hallway, and there was a joyful bark and a large golden retriever came bounding out of the back regions and flung itself at Atholl.

'Allow me to introduce you,' he said. 'This is Shona—she rules the house, I'm afraid!'

Terry looked up at Atholl and laughed, throwing back her head in amusement. 'And I thought Shona was your girlfriend...'

The sun was streaming through the open door and fell on her raised face, catching the gold light in her hair and emphasising her large amber eyes sparkling up at him with amusement, her lips slightly parted. Looking down at her, Atholl felt slightly stunned. He'd realised she was attractive when he'd first seen her. Now he was suddenly conscious that she wasn't just attractive—she was damned beautiful, her eyes like golden sherry set in a sweet heart-shaped face. It unsettled him, made him nervous, thinking again of tattling tongues in the village, trying to matchmake. He'd had enough of that, thank you. He wasn't lonely and he didn't need a relationship with anyone he worked with—not after the last catastrophe.

He flicked a quick look at Terry's bent head as she ruffled the dog's head—the nape of her neck looked slim and vulnerable, her hair curling softly into it. And for a mad moment he imagined bending down and kissing the soft curve of her cheek. He could almost feel the velvety touch of her skin...

He started suddenly, realising that Terry was smiling at him, waiting for him to say something.

'You'll find your room upstairs on the right,' he said gruffly. 'It's a bit basic, but you can dump your things there, freshen up and then do what you like here while I do my visits.'

'Sure,' Terry said. 'But if you'd like me to come with you I'm very happy to.'

'No, that won't be necessary today. Tomorrow will be soon

enough to start work,' he said tersely. 'I'll be off, then. See you later.'

He strode out abruptly and leapt into the Land Rover, revving it up and accelerating out of the little drive with a spurt of pebbles. What the hell was he thinking about, allowing himself to even notice what Terry Younger looked like, let alone visualise himself touching her—and more? How much easier it would have been if the agency had sent a man, or even a much older woman to take the job—anyone but a knockout like Terry Younger.

He pictured her elfin face with those large expressive eyes like liquid gold and the crisp fair hair framing her face. The trouble was, he thought, gripping the steering-wheel tightly, he'd been taken unawares when Terry had come along, imagining that she would be a man. He scowled out at the landscape as he drove along. Just because he'd led a monastic life for the past few months, the last thing he needed was the distraction of sexual attraction with a colleague. Then he smiled grimly to himself. A city girl like her would probably not last long in the remote world of Scuola—after all, it hadn't taken Zara long to find the place was not to her liking.

Terry stood in the doorway, staring after Atholl with a puzzled frown. He seemed to have suddenly become tense, uneasy about something. Was he perhaps regretting offering her the job? She shrugged. It was too late to back out now, and she'd not give up the job without a fight. She bent down to pat Shona, who looked up at her with trusting brown eyes.

'I'll show him, Shona,' she whispered. 'He'll not regret having me in the practice—even if I am a woman.'

CHAPTER THREE

A DOG barking and the sound of horses' hooves on the road woke Terry up with a start from a deep sleep. For a moment she panicked, thinking she was back in London, but there was no sound of traffic and no curtains at the window to cut off the light streaming onto her bed. She relaxed back again. Of course, she was in a little cottage on Scuola—about seven hundred miles away from her old home and quite safe. She searched for her watch on the bedside table and squinted at the face with amazed horror. It was nine-thirty—she must have slept for twelve hours.

Gradually the previous day's events began to unravel through her mind. It had been a day of mixed emotions, leaving her beloved London, meeting Atholl Brodie in the most dramatic of circumstances, then finding out he was the man she was going to be working with.

She lay for a second reflecting on just what kind of a man he was—outspoken, decisive, but probably fair enough in his dealings with people. And, of course, there were his looks... deep blue eyes in a strong good-looking face swam into her mind. She sighed and swung her legs over the bed. Hadn't she learned that drop-dead gorgeous men had too much confidence, things came too easily to them? She was certainly not about to stray into dangerous emotional territory again—especially in a working relationship. But there was a peculiar little flicker of excitement at the thought of seeing him later.

She padded over to the open window and looked out on a brilliant day, catching her breath at the view. The sun was shining on the distant vista of a blue sea she could see over the fields, and just down by the side of the cottage there was a stream that tumbled and sparkled its way under a little bridge and towards a copse. Through the open window drifted the sweet fresh smells of early spring and the sound of the chattering water.

'A far cry from London,' she murmured, peering down to see if Atholl's car had gone from the front of the cottage. There was no sign of it, so he must have gone to work.

There was a scrabbling noise at the door and Shona trotted in, coming over to nuzzle Terry and then lie on her side in a patch of warm sunlight. Terry had a quick wash and threw on some clothes from her case, which Atholl had placed on the small landing. She squinted into the tiny mirror in the darkest corner of the little room as she flicked a brush through her hair. Her image looked back at her—large eyes framed by wayward short curly fair hair. Funny how a slight change in hair colour and cut could make a face look quite different, she thought. She turned to the dog looking up at her with interest.

'Right, Shona, let's see what's for breakfast, shall we?'

The kitchen was a tiny room with just enough space for a sink, fridge and oven. On the working top was a note. 'If you feel rested enough to come to the surgery, please take my uncle's car parked in the layby just down the road. Keys in drawer.'

After a cup of black coffee and a fruitless hunt for anything more sustaining than a stale piece of bread, Terry put on a jacket and made her way to the car.

'Bye, Shona,' she called to the dog, who was watching her through the window. 'If I don't find my way I may be back soon!'

In fact, it was an easy ten-minute drive to The Sycamores. The worst part was parking the car in between a builder's lorry and Atholl's Land Rover in the drive. The house did indeed look rundown, Terry thought, taking a more detailed look at the paintwork on the windows, the battered front door and the small neglected border covered with weeds.

'I could easily make that look better when the flat's ready,' she murmured to herself as she went into the hall.

The waiting room was crowded and there was no one at Reception.

'The doctor's running late—you'll have to wait a wee while,' said an elderly man helpfully, by the door.

'I'm here to work, actually.' Terry smiled, making her way through the room. A battery of eyes watched her go behind the reception counter while she waited for Isobel to materialise. She looked at the disparate crowd of people who gazed curiously back at her. Hopefully soon she would get to know them, and start to feel part of another community.

'Ah, we wondered when you'd make an appearance!' said Isobel, coming into the room with an armful of post.

Terry was getting used to Isobel's forthright manner and pulled a rueful face. 'Sorry I'm late. I had the best sleep I've had in ages, though. Now I'm ready, willing and able…'

Isobel nodded. 'Aye, well, you had reason to be tired, didn't you? Atholl told me about the accident you were involved in yesterday—quite a baptism of fire in your new home!' She pursed her lips. 'And talking of home, did you find anything for breakfast in that fridge of his?'

'Not a lot.' Terry laughed. 'But I'm fine. Fortunately there was plenty of coffee.'

Isobel made a tutting sound. 'I'll get you something soon. No one can work on an empty stomach—any doctor should know that. Now, Atholl says would you use the room at the end of the passage—he'll be through directly to show you how the programme on the computer works and then I'll send your first patient through.'

Terry looked around her new surgery. It was quite a large room with an examining couch at one side, a washbasin and two enormous cupboards on the other, and a window with a crooked blind over it at the end. A bookcase filled with weighty medical tomes and magazines was squeezed near the door. Probably it was normally Euan's room, she surmised. There were a few yellowing photographs on the wall of groups of students, and surely one of Euan himself, a stern white-haired gentleman glaring into the room, looking very like Atholl might do in years to come. She opened a drawer in the desk and smiled when she saw the contents—a lipstick and eyeliner wasn't anything Uncle Euan would have use for. The last locum must have been a woman!

There was a tap at the door and Atholl entered. He looked much smarter than yesterday in a dark suit and tie, his white shirt emphasising his tanned face. From a purely objective point of view, Terry told herself, he certainly was one eye-catching guy.

Atholl's eyes flicked over her, completed a quick survey of her navy trouser suit and the pink silk shirt she was wearing under the jacket. She looked delectable, he thought wryly.

He'd had time to reflect in the last twelve hours on what a fool he'd been yesterday, rushing off rudely like a madman just because he was frightened of a rerun of the situation he'd had with Zara. It wasn't Terry's fault that she was so damned attractive and the poor girl hadn't had a very welcoming reception. If they were going to work well together it was imperative that he maintain a cordial working relationship with her. From now on he'd try and behave sensibly—but keep his distance.

'You slept all right, then?' he asked. 'You'd gone to bed by the time I got back.'

He sounded more relaxed than he had the day before when he'd roared off after depositing her at the cottage, Terry thought with relief.

'Yes, I slept like a log. I'm sorry I was so late. I'd no idea it was halfway through the morning when I woke up.'

He shook his head dismissively. 'It doesn't matter—you were tired.' He gave a rueful grin. 'I'm sorry about the lack of food. Isobel's just been giving me a hard time about that. I'd no time to shop as I was up at the crack of dawn meeting some man from the local health authority who wants us to provide a room for some alternative medicine clinic.'

Terry gathered from his tone that he was totally against that request. She smiled. 'You can buy me a sandwich at lunchtime if you like.'

'I'll do better than that. I've got to take some gear over to the outward bound place before lunch. If you come with me you can meet Pete, his wife and the boys. I'll bring some food and we'll have it on the way back. The quicker you get to know the area the better.'

'Sounds great.'

He bent forward to switch on the computer and said,

'Before I show you the ropes as far as the software we use is concerned, there's a reporter here to speak to you.'

Terry looked surprised. 'Whatever for? What can I have to say to him?'

Atholl smiled. 'It's about your sterling work yesterday in the car accident. It'll make good copy. "New young doctor on Scuola saves baby in car accident."'

'It certainly wasn't just me involved—you were as well. What paper is this?'

'The *Scuola Recorder*—it's just a weekly newssheet about local happenings.'

'I…I don't know if I really want to be featured,' Terry said doubtfully.

He shrugged. 'I know it's a bit of a bore, but they don't have much to talk about here and that's a happy storyline.'

'I suppose…if people are interested.'

'I can assure you that a heart-warming article about a new doctor ensures the patients will be very keen to be seen by you! They're normally a very conservative lot and don't like change.'

Let's hope the story won't spread much further than Scuola, thought Terry. Then shook herself mentally. She'd nothing to fear now, had she? She just had to relax and enjoy her new life.

A few seconds later Atholl ushered in a young gangling lad with red hair and freckles and an eager manner, like a young puppy. He strode towards Terry with his hand held out.

'Hello, there! Ian Brown, *Scuola Recorder*. I just wanted a few moments of your time to get the lowdown on the accident yesterday. I believe you were the heroine of the hour, rescuing a baby from a car?'

Terry flicked a look of embarrassment at Atholl, who was

watching the interview leaning against the wall with his long legs crossed. 'There was nothing heroic about it—and, of course, Dr Brodie was very much involved.'

'It was very dangerous, though. The car could have exploded at any second, isn't that right?' persisted Ian.

'Fortunately all was well.' Terry smiled. 'There really isn't much more to tell. The main thing was that Maisie and little Amy weren't hurt despite the car being badly crushed.'

'Of course, of course…but could I just get a little background info? Where you come from, why you're here…you know the sort of thing?'

Terry smiled brightly. 'Well, I'm from the South of England.' She kept it vague. 'I wanted a change of scene away from the city, somewhere more remote, and Scuola is a beautiful place.'

'So you you've never been here before?'

'No, but it sounded just perfect.'

Ian's cheery face raised a sceptical eyebrow. 'Bit of a risk isn't it? Coming to live here without viewing the place first? Jumping into untested waters, as it were…'

'I'm sure it will work out,' said Terry firmly. She didn't want to answer any more probing questions, because they seemed to bring back with startling clarity the reasons that had forced her to come up to Scotland. She sat down behind her desk. 'Look, I'm afraid I really must get on now. I'm already late for my first day and I know Dr Brodie's very busy.'

The young man looked disappointed. 'Well, at least let me take a photo of you both, perhaps with Dr Brodie welcoming his new colleague to the practice…you know the sort of thing.'

Reluctantly Terry allowed Ian to manoeuvre her beside

Atholl, and he took several photos of them shaking hands and looking rather self-consciously towards the mobile phone on which he'd taken the pictures.

'Good!' he said with satisfaction. 'You're very photo-genic, Dr Younger—they seem to get smashing-looking lady doctors here! That Dr Grahame who was here before was one bonny lass!'

Atholl scowled, not remarking on Ian's observations, and snapped, 'Have you finished, then?'

Terry flicked a glance at Atholl, noting his abrupt change of mood. It had probably been brought on by the cheeky attitude of the young reporter.

'Would you like to see the photo?' enquired Ian, holding up his mobile to her. 'Look, you have to agree, you make a really handsome couple!'

Atholl's expression became even more surly. 'For God's sake, don't start making things up now,' he warned him tersely.

Ian Brown grinned, completely unfazed by Atholl's irrita-tion. 'Don't worry. I'll send you a copy of the article—it'll be a lovely human-interest story! "Doctors to the rescue!" Sounds good, doesn't it?'

Atholl and Terry looked at each other dubiously as Ian gave them a cheery wave and went out of the room.

'Let's hope he doesn't allow his imagination to run away with him,' growled Atholl drily. 'Give the folk round here a little information and they'll have us engaged! It doesn't take much for them to leap to the wrong conclusion.'

'Rumours can fly around on practically no evidence,' agreed Terry. 'It must be hard to keep one's private life to oneself in a small community, I imagine.'

'Too right! My patients can't wait to marry me off, but I've still got my freedom, I'm relieved to say, and I've no plans to change that!'

He sounded quite adamant about it, although Terry couldn't imagine that a man with his looks didn't have a girlfriend somewhere in the background—or, if that wasn't the case, several girls ready to pounce on him if he showed willing! Well, his attitude suited her, because she too was glad that she was fancy-free, free of Max and the way he'd dragged her family down, and ready to concentrate on her work and new life.

She sat down at the desk. 'Now, show me the ins and outs of this system before I see my first patient.'

He sat down beside her and started to explain how things worked.

It had hardly been necessary for young Ian Brown to come and cover the story—every patient Terry had that morning mentioned the accident. News travelled very fast in a small community.

'I'm Maisie's auntie, Doreen Lovatt,' said her first patient, a large, rosy-cheeked woman who limped in slowly with a stick and sat down heavily in the chair opposite Terry. 'Whatever would she have done without you and Dr Brodie?' she began chattily. 'I went to see her last night in the hospital, and she's doing really well, and as for that gorgeous baby… well, it doesn't bear thinking about, does it?'

Terry could see that this consultation could last quite a while if she allowed Mrs Lovatt to discuss her niece's accident and quickly interrupted. 'I'm so glad they're both OK, Mrs Lovatt. Maisie was terribly brave. Now, how can I help you?'

'Well, Doctor, it's my knee. I'm in agony. Years ago I had it, but it's suddenly ballooned up without warning again.'

Mrs Lovatt was equally voluble about her knee, but at least they were on the right subject—the patient's health!

Terry examined the knee and noted how stiff and swollen it was and how painful when moved. She asked Mrs Lovatt if she'd been prescribed any medication for it in the past.

'Oh, no, I don't really like taking tablets, Dr Younger. I'd rather just get by if I can. But it's so bad at the moment I can't look after baby Amy or the other two little ones. That's my job, you see. I'm a childminder and Maisie brings Amy over everyday from the mainland while she works at the news-agent's.'

Terry pondered for a minute, looking at her overweight patient. 'Have you been doing anything out of the ordinary that might have injured the joint?'

Doreen Lovatt blushed. 'Well…you may think it's a bit ri-diculous—a woman of my size—but, having not done any exercise for years, my friend persuaded me to join a dance troupe. We call it "Strictly Formation Dancing". We've been rehearsing a lot lately and perhaps I overdid it a bit.'

The vision this presented of Doreen dancing in a reveal-ing dress was a vivid one, but Terry suppressed a smile and said enthusiastically, 'That's marvellous. What a great idea, and such fun. But that sort of high-impact exercise is probably what's aggravated your knee.'

Doreen's plump face fell. 'I thought you'd say it was that. Will I have to give up the dancing?' she asked dolefully.

'I hope not—but you will have to rest it and let the liga-ments settle down. I'm not sure if the trauma to your knee has given you a flare-up of arthritis. It could even be a displaced cartilage…'

Doreen looked alarmed. 'How can you tell, then, Doctor?'

'If it's arthritis it should settle down after a few days of rest and some anti-inflammatory tablets. I believe a physiotherapist has a session at the hospital so if we could get you an appointment you could be shown a few gentle exercises to keep the muscles in that area toned. If it's still not right after a week or so, we ought to have an MRI scan done so that we can see exactly what's going on.'

Terry looked kindly at the worried-looking woman. 'One thing I'd like you to do that could help…and I don't think you'll find it too difficult when you're taking all this exercise…'

'What's that, Doctor?'

'If you lost some weight it would help your knee a lot—you might find it settles down completely.' Terry put it as gently as she could. She didn't want to hurt this nice woman's feelings.

To her alarm Doreen's face crumpled and she pulled out a hankie from a large handbag and blew her nose noisily. 'Oh, I have tried, really I have, but it's difficult. I've three sons and a husband who all like huge meals, and I can't stop myself eating with them. I know I look a sight.'

Terry leaned over the desk and patted Doreen's plump hand. Doreen might have a cheery face but it obviously hid the very real worry she had about her weight, and the lack of self-esteem she felt probably affected her whole life. And there were many people who felt like she did, too embarrassed to ask for help.

'You don't look a sight, Doreen, far from it,' she said gently. 'My only concern is for your health. Extra pounds put strain on your body—blood pressure, joints and the risk of diabetes. I don't want you to stop eating with your family, Doreen, just not quite so much.'

'I've got no willpower,' said Doreen mournfully.

'Look, I'm going to suggest I hold a weekly weigh-in at the surgery to try and encourage people who need to lose weight. That and a diet sheet should help your resolve.' She smiled at Doreen. 'You're the first patient I've seen in my new job, so I really want my first patient to do well! Will you come?'

Doreen looked brighter. 'Yes—yes, I'd like that, something to keep me on the straight and narrow. Actually, there's one or two of us in the troupe that are a bit weighty, so they might come along as well!'

She limped out quite happily and when she got to the door she turned and said cryptically, 'It's good to have a sympathetic lady doctor at last—someone who's main interest is in her patients and hasn't got other things on her mind. Well, you know what I mean, Dr Younger.'

What exactly *did* she mean? wondered Terry as she tapped in her notes for Doreen Lovatt. Perhaps when she knew Isobel better she'd make discreet enquiries about this woman that had been the locum before her.

The morning sped by with the usual variety of ills that presented themselves at a GP's surgery, from chronic backache to glue ear in a small child. And all the patients were keen to talk about Maisie and her accident, which Terry surmised probably added at least half an hour to the morning's work.

Just as she was about to shut down the computer, Isobel put her head round the door.

'Bad news, I'm afraid,' she said grimly.

'Oh, dear…what?' asked Terry, wondering if Isobel ever came in looking happy.

Isobel's voice sank to a conspiratorial whisper. 'Cyril Rathbone—that's the bad news! He haunts this place. I told him surgery was finished but he won't take no for an answer.

Always thinks he's at death's door and has to be seen immediately. Mind you,' she acknowledged, 'he and his wife make
a wonderful job of running the Caledonian Hotel up the hill
and I think that's quite stressful. Shall I send him in?'

'No problem,' said Terry with a grin. 'There's at least one
in every practice!' Whatever Isobel said about this patient, this
could be the one time he was really ill after all.

Mr Rathbone, short, bald, but nattily dressed, marched into
the room. 'Thank you for seeing me, Doctor,' he said briskly.
'I normally see Dr Euan Brodie—we're old friends, sit on the
same committees, that sort of thing. He keeps a very good eye
on me but, of course, he's not available, which is a nuisance.'

Terry smiled, noting with amusement the way he'd made
it clear that he was a special patient of the practice! 'How can
I help you, Mr Rathbone?'

'I didn't want to bother you really, but I'm in such pain
that my wife insisted I should come and see *someone,*
whoever it was…'

'I see. I hope I can give as much satisfaction as Dr Brodie.'

Her sarcasm was lost on a man like Mr Rathbone, and she
wondered, with his brusque manner, how he managed to make
such a success of his hotel. Perhaps he was completely different with his guests!

'Well, of course you don't know me like old Dr Brodie,'
he said tersely. 'He's a wonderful diagnostician.'

Meaning you don't have any faith in me at all, thought
Terry wryly. But she sympathised. The patient-doctor relationship was a very personal thing built over a long time, and
seeing someone new could be daunting.

'The thing is, I've got an excruciating blister on my toe,'
continued Mr Rathbone. 'I know they can become infected

very easily and turn to septicaemia, so I'd like an antibiotic to fight the infection.'

'Let me have a look at it,' said Terry. 'Take off your shoe and sock.'

'There!' exclaimed Mr Rathbone dramatically, revealing his foot with a small red patch on his little toe. 'Can you wonder I can hardly walk?' He took out a folded-up newspaper from his jacket pocket and handed it to Terry, pointing out an underlined headline with a stubby finger. 'Read that! It's all about diabetes and how an injury can be deadly if left untreated if you have that condition.'

Of all the things that could irritate a doctor, reflected Terry, it's when a patient quoted something they've read about a condition and assume they've got it!

She looked through his notes on the computer carefully—there was no history of diabetes or any other existing condition that might make the area on his toe a cause for concern.

'I see you had a blood and urinary test for diabetes a short time ago,' she said. 'They all proved negative, so I don't think we need worry about that.'

'I thought I'd just check that you were aware of the complications should I have had it,' replied Mr Rathbone. 'One can't be too careful.'

Terry bit back the urge to say, *But one can be incredibly irritating!* and said instead, 'It must be rather sore. It's obviously been rubbing on shoes that are too tight. The best thing would be to put surgical spirit on it to harden the skin and a small padded plaster over the affected part. And, of course, wear soft shoes like slippers, if your normal ones hurt, until it's healed.'

'Slippers?' echoed Mr Rathbone incredulously. 'I run a

hotel—I can hardly stroll around in front of my guests looking sloppy! What about antibiotics? Surely I ought to have a course of them?'

'I think we'll keep them as a last resort, Mr Rathbone. Hopefully it won't become infected if you do as I suggest. But do come back if it gets worse.'

Terry's voice was pleasant but very firm—she wasn't going to be bullied into giving him medicine he didn't need. Mr Rathbone stared at her in disbelief, then shook his head sadly. 'I only hope you know what you're doing—you young doctors are so inexperienced. You're not from around here, are you?'

He got up and walked with a pronounced limp to the door before turning round and saying dourly, 'I don't know what's happened to this practice—I see a different person every time I come. Where's the other woman that was here? Not that I had much faith in her, her mind didn't seem to be on the job at all!' He looked scornfully at Terry. 'I suppose you'll be gone soon too—there's just no continuity!'

He went out and Terry blew out her cheeks in amazement, feeling a mixture of irritation and amusement.

'Perhaps he'll see Atholl next time,' she murmured, although she'd be surprised if a man like Atholl would let Mr Rathbone dictate to him. She stretched and yawned, putting the man out of her head. She was ready for that picnic lunch that Atholl had promised after they'd met his friend and the boys.

Atholl had changed out of his smart suit and had on jeans and an old plaid lumber jacket. He looked critically at Terry's outfit.

'It could be cold when we get to the loch, it's right up in the hills.' he said. 'I always keep a spare set of warm and casual clothes here to change into in case I'm called out to a mountain rescue or somewhere that doesn't require that suit I wear for meetings.' He rummaged in the boot of the Land Rover and threw a fleece over to her. 'Wear that when we get there and you should be OK.'

Shona was in the back of the car, leaping about in excitement. 'I just picked her up when I was called out this morning,' Atholl explained. 'I often do that. Some of my elderly patients love seeing her and she enjoys being made a fuss of.'

Terry could imagine what pleasure the lovely dog would give to lonely old people—and a great source of interest to them. 'I've always wanted a dog,' she said, 'but inner-city London wasn't the place to keep one.'

'So did you have a flat or a house in London?' he enquired as they set off towards the hills.

'A flat,' she replied briefly.

'And was it near your work?'

'Fairly—I could walk there.' Her brisk tone didn't encourage further questions.

Terry wasn't very informative about her life in London, Atholl reflected. The way she'd reacted to the young reporter, the guarded way she'd answered his questions...it all added up to someone who wanted to forget her life there. He'd hazard a guess that she'd had an unhappy affair...she wouldn't be the first person to move because of a broken heart. Oddly the thought of Terry in love with an unknown man made him uneasy—though someone as stunning as her must have had hordes of men longing to take her out. He accelerated rather fast up the road that led into the hills, large capable hands on the steering-wheel, intrigued and slightly irritated by this little mystery. He'd find out soon enough, he thought.

'And how did you find your surgery today?' he asked. 'Although I guess ailments are pretty universal.'

'I enjoyed it. Maisie's aunt, Doreen Lovatt, came in to see me with a bad knee but we ended up talking about her worries over her weight.'

'Ah, Doreen—she's a good woman. In fact, all of her family are a bit overweight—you should see her husband and three sons.'

'Poor woman. I tried to persuade her to lose some weight, but I can see it might be difficult for her. I wondered if you'd mind if I had a trial weight clinic for a few weeks? Say, after surgery one evening?'

Atholl flicked an amused glance at her. 'Trying to improve the lifestyle on Scuola already? But feel free to do that if you wish—in fact, I think it's a good idea. There's quite a few would benefit around here.'

They continued talking in a general way about the practice and Terry mentioned Mr Rathbone.

'There always seems to be someone who's very demand-ing in every practice,' she commented.

'Absolutely.' He grinned. 'But the day you ignore them, that's the day their severe stomach cramps really do turn out to be appendicitis. Mind you, he and his wife have trans-formed the hotel they run. It was in a terrible state a few years ago when they bought it, and by sheer hard work they've given it a complete makeover and it's a real asset to the area. However, I don't know how Janet Rathbone stands him.'

'Apparently she insisted he come and see us.'

'To get him out of her hair I should think.' Atholl laughed. 'No doubt we'll see him again next week. By the way, I ought to fill you in a bit about the four lads you're going to meet.

They come from the same area that I grew up in, all from broken families. I don't think any of them have had much notice taken of them individually or had the chance to do anything but get into trouble—they've all had run-ins with the police. These few weeks are meant to give them a breath of air, an opportunity to put their energies to good use.'

'That's a great idea. Who started it?'

'Pete and I,' Atholl said drily. 'You see, we were exactly the same at their age—out of control and getting sucked into gangs and dodgy company. We were lucky. We managed to get away from it all just in time, and now we want to give others that chance as well.'

'That's a great thing to do,' she said quietly.

There was more to Atholl Brodie than good looks, then— he was someone who'd made the grade despite a tough start and was prepared to help other youngsters. A flicker of bitterness reminded Terry how different Atholl was from Max, who'd used his good looks and intelligence to such ill effect, hurting so many in his wake.

She flicked a look at Atholl's strong profile and sighed. If only she'd met someone like him two years ago—someone who was kind, generous with his time, concerned for others. Instead, she thought bitterly, she'd been hoodwinked by honeyed words and her own gullibility—as had her father, she reflected. She wondered if she would she ever believe in a man again or trust her own judgement.

Atholl turned off the road up an unmade cart track, bumping over the holes until they came to a barn-like building in front of a small loch surrounded by hills. A washing line hung outside with several pairs of jeans and T-shirts hanging from it.

'This is The Culleens where Pete and his wife have their outward bound venture,' he remarked. 'You'll like Sally— she's a great girl and expecting their first baby in about five weeks. She supervises most of the domestic stuff and Pete's the outward bound expert.'

He opened the car door and jumped out. 'Better put on that fleece—you'll need it here,' he advised.

He opened the rear door and Shona flung herself out and raced madly away towards the back of the building, barking excitedly. Terry followed Atholl as a burly young man wearing a thick sweater came into view from behind the barn. The man lifted his hand and hailed Atholl.

'Hello, there!' he called. 'I was hoping you'd come.'

Atholl turned to Terry. 'Let me introduce you to Pete Brown. Pete, Terry Younger, our new locum at the practice and assistant here.'

Terry smiled, seeing the familiar look of surprise when she was introduced to anyone. 'No,' she said quickly. 'I'm not a man! I know you were expecting one, but I'm afraid you'll have to make do with me!'

Pete grinned and shook her hand in a crushing grip. 'I can tell you're a lass all right!' He turned round and bellowed, 'Sally! Sally! Come here and meet Atholl's new locum! Terry Younger...'

A tall and very pregnant-looking girl wearing jeans and an old coat came out of the barn. 'Hi, there! Lovely to meet you, Terry.' She had a wide, attractive smile and Terry took to her immediately. 'It'll be great to have a woman to talk to some-times instead of all these men!'

'Talking of which, you'd better come and meet these boys,' Pete said. 'They're doing well on the whole—only Zac's not pulling his weight at the moment, and yet he was very keen to start with.'

He led the way round the side of the building where three large youths were chopping wood whilst one leant against the wall watching them, his jaws working rhythmically as he chewed gum. The other boys stopped what they were doing and watched as Atholl and Terry came up to them.

'Right, lads, meet Terry,' said Pete. 'She's a GP in Atholl's practice and she'll be with us on some of our activities.'

The boy leaning against the wall leered at Terry suggestively. 'Don't mind being overseen by her…'

'Watch it, Zac,' warned Pete sharply. 'Try and be courteous.' He turned to Terry. 'Let me introduce you to Bert, Len, Colin and Zac.'

The boys nodded to her, slightly warily, possibly aware that they were being assessed by this new woman. Terry nodded back. She wasn't going to be effusive about meeting them—it could seem patronising.

'I'm looking forward to seeing you abseiling,' she said. 'I've never done it myself.'

'You coming with us when we do that?' asked one of the boys. 'You could try it then.'

Pete nodded. 'Yes, starting with a trek across the moor and maybe some kayaking as well.'

'Sounds fun,' said Terry.

Zac laughed heartily. 'You wait till you see us—we're bloody hopeless.'

'Why aren't you helping to cut the wood, Zac?' asked Atholl.

Zac shrugged. 'Ask Pete—he says I'm a danger to everyone. I'm quite happy to watch, mind you.' He gave another robust laugh.

'You're just a bit clumsy, Zac,' remarked Pete. 'You nearly lost a finger cutting the bread yesterday—I can't risk you using an axe until that cut's healed.'

Zac giggled. 'I was hungry—did it a bit quickly.'

Pete shook his head in mock despair. 'You're always hungry, Zac, you've an appetite like a horse. I hope you've brought some more basics, Atholl, to keep this lot fed.'

'There's a load of bread, milk and meat in the Land Rover, as well as all the gear I promised you, like ropes and tents. Perhaps the lads could unload the stuff now and take it in,' said Atholl. Terry frowned and looked at Zac closely. He had reddened eyes and his lips were dry and cracked, and some-thing about his slightly manic manner reminded her of some of the kids who'd been patients of hers in London. She watched as the boys carried the gear from Atholl's car to a shed by the barn, Zac's whoops of laughter drifting towards them. She would mention it to Atholl later. They went into the converted barn which was divided simply into various rooms—a large kitchen and sitting area, two dormitory-type bedrooms and a bathroom.

'Are you enjoying yourselves?' Terry asked the three boys who had come in with them. Zac had wandered off to throw sticks in the air for Shona to run after.

'Aye, it's good,' said one of them. 'But we miss the telly. We're only allowed an hour a day.'

'If you behave, that is,' said Pete with a grin. 'Right, lads, you start making the lunch. What is it, Sally?'

'We'll have spaghetti bolognaise with grated cheese on top, bread and fruit,' said Sally, turning to Atholl and Terry. 'Are you going to have some with us?'

'Thanks, but not today, Sally,' said Atholl. 'I'm just giving

Terry a mini-tour of the area before we do some visits this afternoon, but we'll be on duty when you do the abseiling.'

'That'll be great.' Sally smiled. 'Better bring your waterproofs! And thanks for delivering the extra provisions—just what was needed!'

Atholl whistled for Shona, who came bounding up happily to them and jumped into the Land Rover. Zac followed and stood watching them stolidly, still chewing gum, his arms folded.

'Go and help your friends make your lunch,' suggested Atholl as he got back into the car and started the engine.

Zac gave that extravagant laugh again, kicked a stone and ambled back towards the barn.

'The boys really seem to have relaxed since they've come here—and they've got stuck into doing things. When they arrived they were sullen and uncooperative,' remarked Atholl as he drove back down the winding road. 'Only Zac seems to have slowed down almost to a full stop.'

'His manner reminded me of some of the patients I used to see in London,' began Terry. 'It makes me wonder if—'

'He's on something?' put in Atholl, turning to her with a wry smile. 'I have to say he seemed a bit hyper.'

Terry looked at Atholl, surprised at his perception. 'Exactly! I've seen it before—the slightly reddened eyes, that excitable laughter. And didn't Pete say he had a huge appetite? All could be indicators of cannabis.'

'It did occur to me as well—I'll speak to Pete about it tonight. The boys all receive post from time to time and although Pete and Sally try to keep a strict eye on the lads, it's something that you could miss in the early stages.' His periwinkle-blue eyes twinkled at her, dark hair flopping over his forehead, and suddenly a flicker of attraction caught her by surprise, flashing through her body like lightning through a conductor. 'Same old problems even in little Scuola, eh?' he said.

'Absolutely,' she agreed, slightly flustered at her reaction to him.

He changed gear as the car started to labour up a steep hill. 'Anyway let's forget about Zac for a while. I want to show you a favourite place of mine—perfect for having a bite to eat. It's good to get away from the surgery for a while.'

It was ridiculous the way her heart began thumping at the thought of being alone with Atholl, thought Terry. He was a work colleague, for heaven's sake, and the last thing she needed was to fall for another man's charms so easily!

CHAPTER FOUR

THEY had been driving away from the loch and gradually getting higher where the terrain was rougher, and now Atholl turned into a small clearing where a circle of silver birches made a pretty glade overlooking the countryside and the sea between Scuola and the mainland. He shot a look at his watch.

'Just time for lunch and a quick coffee.'

He got out of the car and stretched, his lean strong body looking like an advertisement for some impossibly marvellous health food, and again there was that sudden flutter like captured butterflies trying to escape from Terry's stomach as she watched him.

He held her shoulders and turned her towards the Scuola Sound, and she felt herself tense at his touch. He was much taller than she, dominating her petite form, acting as a windbreak between her and the freezing wind whipping through the trees.

'Look, from here it's a good vantage point to show you where the surgery is in relation to the rest of the island—do you see it?'

'Oh…yes, yes, I can. It's a wonderful view.' Her throat felt a little dry and her voice came out rather breathlessly.

One hand still held her shoulder and with the other he pointed to a small steamer crossing the firth, bending so that his eyeline was the same height as hers, his face very close to her cheek.

'And there goes the *Highland Lady*—a luxury cruise for some lucky people round the islands,' he said. 'They'll probably be sitting down to a fine lunch of lobster and champagne right now.' He grinned down at her. 'Nothing like that here, I'm afraid. It's all rather basic stuff—oat cakes, local baps, cheese, ham and smoked salmon. Take your pick.'

He went over to the car and hauled a basket out of the boot and Terry relaxed slightly. Having him quite so near seemed to be doing devastating things to her mind and body—something she hadn't bargained for at all.

'It all looks delicious,' she said brightly. 'I didn't expect so much. When did you buy it?'

He laughed. 'Isobel did the buying! She doesn't trust me to get the right stuff.' The sound of a ship's siren hooted mournfully over to them and he turned and pointed through the trees. 'Look down there again—you can see where the ferry comes in, and it's clear enough to see where the car rammed into the dock wall when you arrived. And follow the road round and beyond the curve of the hill is the hospital.'

The wind had become even stronger and colder and, despite wearing the fleece, Terry felt chilled as she looked down.

'Lord, this really is Highland weather,' she said, wrapping the fleece more tightly around her slight figure. 'I'm glad of your fleece.'

He laughed and poured some steaming coffee from a Thermos flask into a mug and put it on the ground. 'I told you, you've got to be tough to work here.' He looked at her critically. 'You need to be better clothed for these climes. Let me feel your hands. Good God, they're freezing!' He started to rub them between his warm ones, then took off his scarf and put it round her neck, tying it into a loose knot. He looked down at her with a smile. 'There! That's what's needed!'

What was needed, thought Terry nervously, was for Atholl Brodie to remove his strapping body away from hers. No wonder her pulse had gone into overdrive... Perhaps it was because they were out in the clear fresh air of the outdoors but that treacherous attraction seemed determined to come flickering back, and it was very easy to imagine cuddling up to his chest and out of the biting wind.

What was she like? she thought angrily to herself. Was she so needy that she had to indulge in pipe dreams with a man she had only just met? A man, moreover, who had no time for women—just as she, of course, had no time for men after the way they'd destroyed her life in London.

'Thank you,' she said, stepping back from the danger zone that was Atholl Brodie. 'I'm dying for some coffee, and this food looks delectable. I can't wait to eat it. Everything tastes twice as good in the open air.'

Atholl laughed. 'Hardly cordon bleu!'

As they started to eat, he pointed out the little island of Hersa across Scuola Sound, to the left of the mainland. Far away they could see the ferry, a small craft in the glittering blue sea, making its way back to the dock. Then Atholl pointed up to the sky.

'Look,' he whispered. 'Hovering just to the right of us—a kestrel. Isn't that a wonderful sight?'

She watched as the bird fluttered and then plunged like an arrow to the ground not far from them, and she smiled at Atholl in delight. 'Do you know, I've never seen that before.'

The wind whipped her hair into a halo round her head and

her eyes were sparkling with the pleasure of seeing the beautiful bird. Quite often Terry seemed to have an aura of sadness about her, but in that instant Atholl suddenly saw a beautiful woman filled with a spontaneous enjoyment of life, a joy in the beauty of things—and a shiver of something akin to longing went through him. Terry had the capacity make someone very happy, he reflected. She was good company and, of course, she was damned attractive. It had been a long, long time since he'd met anyone like her.

The expression in his eyes intensified as his gaze swept over her neat figure then rested on her face, and under his scrutiny Terry felt the hairs on the back of her neck stand up. The last thing she'd been thinking of when she'd landed on Scuola was the possibility that there might be drop-dead gorgeous guys on the island like Atholl, and now he seemed to be doing things to her insides that she hadn't felt for a long time—and certainly didn't want to feel!

Atholl wrenched his eyes away from her and moistened his lips. He felt shaken at the total unexpectedness of the attraction he felt for her. Damn it, this was something he hadn't planned. He wanted a quiet life where he could do his work, enjoy his fishing and walking, and he didn't want any distractions from females. That was why he was so bewildered at his reaction because he had the uneasy feeling that if they'd known each other for longer, he'd have taken her in his arms and kissed her soft lips and that little hollow in her neck, and to hell with it being dangerous and getting himself involved in a relationship...

The sound of a bus changing gear noisily as it went up the road brought Atholl back to the present. He took a deep breath and began to pick up the mugs and the Thermos flask. This whole thing was completely crazy. The woman had arrived only yesterday and already he was putting himself in a vulnerable position, allowing himself to be beguiled by a lovely woman. He'd had enough of women to last a lifetime, he thought irritably. It had to be just a spurious attraction, nothing more, a thing of the moment. Keep your distance, Brodie, he growled inwardly to himself.

He put the picnic things in the boot and looked at Terry as she walked towards the car. She was totally different to Zara, yet in one respect they were similar—both had been born to privilege and a world away from the mean streets of the poverty-stricken area he'd come from. They were town girls and he and Terry had very little in common—and he was pretty confident that after a few weeks she would find island life too dull, too isolated and go back to the city, just like Zara.

'It's getting late,' he remarked lightly. 'We'd better get back.'

Terry remained still for a second, wondering if Atholl had felt any spark between them, just as she had. An unfamiliar feeling of excitement that she hadn't felt for so long seemed to glimmer reluctantly into life again like a small bright flame. Then she dismissed the feeling crossly. She was here to give all her attention to work—and through circumstances she'd been given the chance to do just that.

Over the next few days Terry met all the staff at The Sycamores. Bunty was Isobel's part-time assistant, as jolly as Isobel was dour, and Sue was the community nurse, a pleasant woman with three young sons who seemed to be always in trouble at school. The practice shared a manager, Jonathon Murie, with another group of GPs on the mainland and he came over once a week for a practice meeting.

The staff were friendly and relaxed with her, although

there had been the familiar double-take when she'd been introduced to them and Bunty had exclaimed in surprise, 'Oh, we didn't think we'd get a female doctor again!' And the others looked at each other meaningfully. When she knew them better, vowed Terry, she would ask them what all these cryptic references to the previous locum meant!

It was the start of another busy day and there had been a quick meeting before work regarding the ongoing building work at The Sycamores. Atholl came into the office behind Reception, looking harassed, and flung some papers on the table in the back office.

'Wouldn't you know it? The damn builders have found some subsidence on that wall with the damp in it, so it's going to take even longer to complete the job. I dare say they'll be here for months…'

Not what she wanted to hear, Terry reflected. That would surely mean the flat at The Sycamores wouldn't be ready for ages and she would have to stay at Atholl's for longer. Despite her vow to make her job her priority, her mind seemed to dwell rather too much on Atholl. Living in such close proximity to him, she couldn't help but be aware of his physical closeness—when she passed him on the narrow little stairs, and when she lay in bed at night, knowing that he was only a few feet away from her in his room. It didn't take much for her lively imagination to picture his muscled, well-toned body lying on the bed. She felt vaguely ashamed of herself.

Luckily, many evenings he had been at meetings or going over to the mainland hospital to see his uncle, so she was able to have some time to herself. There was no doubt about it, however, the time had come for her to get her own place—and fast. She would speak to him about it over the weekend.

'So I've still got to keep all that junk in my room while the builders are here?' asked Sue Calder, the community nurse, with a grimace. 'It's very squashed in there when there's a mother and her children in for vaccinations.'

'I'm sorry, Sue, I do sympathise. If we could make some more room, I would,' said Atholl.

'What about the room I'm using?' suggested Terry. 'It's very big and I don't need all that space, so perhaps we could move some of the stuff near the bookcase where there's a recess—I suppose it was a fireplace once.'

'You sure about that?' asked Atholl. 'We'd tried to keep your room clutter free so as not to frighten off any new locum.'

She smiled. 'No problem. I'm not put off by clutter. In fact, there already are quite a few old files and books in there which perhaps we could get rid of to make more space. Would that help, Sue?'

Sue grinned. 'I'll say. I've practically had patients sitting on my knee to have their BPs taken. Thanks, Terry, it'll certainly help. By the way, have you two seen the local paper? You've got it, haven't you, Bunty?'

Bunty handed Terry a newspaper with an impish smile. 'You'll probably get a film contract out of this! Talk about Superman and his mate!'

Terry stared at an enormous photograph of her and Atholl grinning into the camera, big headlines proclaiming, 'Doctor Duo Defy Danger—Mother and Baby Saved!'

'For heaven's sake!' she said in amusement. 'That's a bit dramatic!'

Atholl peered over her shoulder at it and snorted derisively, 'That young reporter's gone over the top.'

It was actually a very good photo. Atholl looked like

someone out of a TV medical drama, Terry reflected, his tall frame looking even bigger beside her dainty figure. She folded the paper and slipped it into her bag—just as a memento, she told herself.

The phones started ringing as soon as Isobel put the lines through at eight-thirty. Sue picked up her bag and some patients' notes.

'I'll be going out to see the Mackie sisters this morning,' she said to Atholl. 'They're both so frail that I feel they're going to need some help very soon—but I know for sure they'll resist any suggestions of that! I wonder if you'd drop by when you've time and give me your assessment of the situation. And don't forget to bring your dog—they've a whole tin of biscuits for her!'

'Will do. Perhaps I can fit it in tomorrow or the day after,' agreed Atholl. He turned to Terry. 'It might be quite a good idea if you were to come with me—I'd like to introduce the sisters to you, and show you where they live.'

He started to leave her room, then hesitated, looking back at her. 'I'm out tonight, seeing my uncle at the mainland hospital again, and I won't be back until later.' He smiled, a warm twinkly smile that did devastating things to her heart-beat. 'And thanks for sacrificing a bit of space in your room—much appreciated.'

Terry walked to her room and pushed the newspaper cutting into a drawer, then went to the window, flicking aside the crooked Venetian blind for a second and looking out of the window at the spectacular view across the Scuola Sound. How lucky she was to have found such a gem of a place to work in. The unhappiness she'd felt in the last months in London was receding and every day she felt more relaxed and happy here. Of course, she did have bad moments when she missed the friends that she was unlikely to see for a long time, but gradually a general warm kind of happiness had crept in that she hadn't felt for so long, and everyone at work was so nice to her.

Through the window she watched Atholl walk toward his car, stopping to talk to an elderly patient, his tall frame bending forward to listen to her. Terry smiled wryly to herself. She had to admit that part of her happiness was to do with the strange effect Atholl was having on her.

Silly woman, she chided herself. She had to stamp this feeling out quickly. After all, the last thing she wanted was to get involved with a man again, and Atholl seemed very happy to be a bachelor!

She looked up as Bunty knocked at the door and came in with a list of patients for the morning's surgery.

'Here you go. First off you've got Cyril Rathbone,' she said cheerily. 'His weekly appointment, I suppose.'

'I did seem him a week or two ago,' Terry acknowledged. 'I'll just bring up his notes and then call him in.'

On the face of it he seemed to be one of the 'worried well'—someone convinced that they were ill despite constant reassurance. There had to be some deep underlying insecurity there that led to him using the surgery as a kind of crutch, Terry thought. Perhaps it was the stress of his work. She pressed the button that activated the call screen in the waiting room and after a few seconds Cyril Rathbone appeared.

He cleared his throat and said rather gruffly, 'I…I've not come about myself this time.'

Terry tried not to look too surprised, and he continued, 'It's my wife, she's not well. I know she's not herself, but she won't make an appointment to see anybody—never wants to make a fuss.'

She sounded the complete opposite of her husband, reflected Terry. She leaned forward. 'What makes you think she's not well, Mr Rathbone?'

He looked down at his hands, as if undecided how to describe his wife's symptoms, then said reluctantly, 'It's, well…she seems to get everything wrong. She used to be so efficient. We're in the hotel business and recently the amount of times she's been to the wholesalers and come back with the wrong things on the list is incredible. And she's so clumsy, knocking things over, and then scraping the car going out of the drive innumerable times. The fact is, Doctor…' His voice sank to a conspiratorial whisper, and he looked round as if someone might be listening to them. 'The fact is, I'm beginning to think she drinks—secretly, mind. In our business that would be fatal.'

'Do you smell drink on her breath?'

'No, but it could be vodka—you can't detect that, can you?'

Terry wondered how long ago it had been since Cyril and his wife had had a real heart to heart—it sounded as if they were pretty remote from each other.

'Are you sure you can't get her to come to the surgery? It would be easier. I will come and see her at the hotel if you like but she may refuse to see me if she hasn't requested a visit.'

Cyril shook his head. 'I'm afraid she's not very amenable to my suggestions, and she's always been dead set against anything to do with the medical profession. I can't understand it.'

It would seem inexplicable to him, thought Terry with an inward smile. 'Look, I've got an idea,' she said. 'We're doing a blood-pressure check on all the over-fifties during the next few weeks. Everyone over that age will be invited along, including yourself and your wife. Why don't you suggest you come as a couple as you would prefer someone with you when you have yours done? I could then use the opportunity to ask her in general terms how she feels.'

Mr Rathbone nodded. 'Yes, she might do that. It's a good idea.' He got up from his chair slowly and said with a certain hesitancy, 'The fact is, Doctor, my wife's never been ill in her life—I can't ever remember her complaining about not feeling well. And I suppose it's just come home to me that I'd have to cope if she was laid low.'

And you're frightened, surmised Terry. For the first time perhaps he was beginning to realise how much he relied on her.

'I'm sure you'd be a tower of strength,' said Terry bracingly. 'In the meantime, try not to worry and I'll probably see you in about two weeks.'

It was amazing how comforting the familiar platitudes could be. Cyril even managed a grateful smile as he went out, and the confident and rather arrogant manner he'd had the first time Terry had met him had gone.

At the end of the morning's surgery Terry went into the office and poured herself a cup of coffee before she tackled the blood test and biopsy results via the e-mails she'd had that day. Isobel was speaking on the phone, looking grimmer than ever. She looked up at Terry.

'Atholl had best get down the glen quickly,' she said, putting the phone down. 'Hamish Stoddard has collapsed in a field there and his dogs won't let anyone near him.'

'What about the ambulance? Anyone called it?'

Isobel pursed her lips. 'Oh, yes, but it's got stuck in the mud and they could do with help anyway, getting it out. It's pouring with rain out there, by the way.'

Atholl had strolled in, also to get a coffee, and raised his eyes to the ceiling when he heard the news. 'Oh, God, poor old Hamish. I bet the man's having a heart attack—he's got a history of angina. I'd better take the Land Rover and get there pronto.' He snatched some biscuits from the plate by the coffee. 'I'll take some of these to distract those bad-tempered dogs of his.' He turned to Terry. 'Fancy having your first taste of rural excitement? If you've got wellies and a mac, put them on and come with me—I may need help.'

Caught up with the potential drama of the situation, Terry rushed out of the room to collect her outdoor clothing, a little buzz of anticipation zipping through her at the thought of working closely with Atholl, and that old familiar rush of nervous adrenaline that a medical drama produced.

The weather had changed yet again and Terry gazed out of the car window at the lashing rain. The trees in the fields bent in the wind, and dark clouds scudded across leaden skies, with the background shapes of black mountains. How snug the inside of the car seemed, cocooned from the weather, and how aware she was of the closeness of Atholl sitting next to her. He peered through the windscreen as the wipers did their best to cope with the deluge. It was like driving underwater.

'Nothing like coping with a heart attack in the middle of a field in the pouring rain,' he commented grimly. 'As I said, Hamish has a history of cardiac trouble and he's a heavy smoker, so it's been a disaster waiting to happen. I've been on at him to retire, but he's a stubborn old fool and won't countenance it. These sheep farmers won't give up easily.'

He swung the vehicle in through the rough track to some farm buildings and a group of men huddled round an ambulance at the far end of the field.

'Here we are,' he said. 'Let's see what we can do for him.'

Atholl grabbed his medical bag and they both leapt out of the car and went as quickly as they could through the muddy field to where the ambulance was. And she'd thought she was coming to a quiet little corner of Britain where nothing much happened, reflected Terry wryly. She was beginning to understand what Atholl had meant when he said she'd probably be dealing with a completely different range of situations from the practice in London!

The elderly man was lying on the ground and two sheepdogs were standing guard by him with a small group of men—farm workers and paramedics—grouped beyond him. The ambulance was heavily bedded into the mud—it looked as if it would need a tractor to pull it out.

'You won't get near Hamish,' said one of the men. 'Those bloody dogs just keep going for us every time we get near him.'

'I know them only too well,' said Atholl grimly. 'They're called Whisky and Brandy, and, believe me, that's what you need when you've dealt with them…but at least they know me. Let's see if we can distract them with these biscuits. Have any of you got belts we can use as leads?'

Two of the men took off belts and Atholl gave the dogs some biscuits to tempt them away from their master, then he edged his way towards the stricken man. Terry swallowed hard, taking in the unpromising situation—a man with an acute myocardial infarction in the middle of a field with rain lashing down, an ambulance stuck up to its axis in thick mud and two mad dogs baring their teeth at them. It couldn't get much more dramatic than this, surely?

'Terry, follow closely behind me and we'll take it slowly towards Hamish. I don't want to upset these dogs more than they already are. Bill, do your best to keep them back from us while I listen to his heart.'

Hamish was lying on his back, his colour a chalky grey as he laboured to take breaths.

'The pain…' he gasped, plucking at the neck of his jumper. 'It…it's crushing me…'

Atholl dropped to his knees beside the stricken man. 'We're here to help you, Hamish,' he said calmly. 'And we'll give you something for the pain.'

Both doctors were doing a quick assessment of the man's situation, noting his pallor and the faint sheen of perspiration on his brow. Terry crouched down and took Hamish's hand in one of hers, putting her other on his forehead and feeling the clamminess of his skin. He had to be reassured and calmed, to feel he was in safe hands even if he could hardly take in what she was saying. The all-consuming pain across his chest would be like steel bars compressing him, impairing his ability to breathe. She bent down close to his ear.

'You'll be OK, Hamish. Don't try and talk.'

Hamish mumbled something, his frightened eyes staring at her, although somewhere in the back of his mind and through the crushing pain was the comforting feeling of Terry's hand holding his. She watched as Atholl pulled up Hamish's shabby jumper to listen to his labouring heart through his stethoscope, and laid two fingers on the side of his neck. Atholl's eyes met hers and he shook his head slightly as he heard the heart giving off the irregular thudding of ventricular fibrillation as the lower chambers of the heart contracted rapidly out of beat.

'Get the oxygen from the ambulance,' he shouted to the paramedics through the heavy rain and the frantic barking of the two dogs trying to get round the men fending them off the patient.

Two men staggered over with an oxygen cylinder, slipping and sliding in the mud, and Terry took the attached mask and placed it over the man's face. She watched Atholl slip the cover from a syringe he'd taken from his bag.

'I'm giving him ten thousand units of heparin split into two doses,' he said. 'I don't want to give it to him all at once and start a massive bleed. We also need some Xylocard. It's in the pack—can you get it into him?'

'Yup,' said Terry. 'Four mils, OK?' She pulled the syringe from the pack, checking it was the right one, then pushed the needle firmly into Hamish's upper arm muscle, giving him the full dose of the local anaesthetic.

'Let's hope that does the trick,' muttered Atholl.

Sounding more confident than she felt, Terry said reassuringly, 'Xylocard's very effective in settling an unstable heart rhythm.'

Although Hamish Stoddard probably didn't realise it at the moment, he was one lucky patient, she thought. Atholl had obviously had great experience with cardiac attacks. She watched his expression as he listened intently to the man's chest after the injection.

'How is it?' she asked, her voice tense.

Atholl closed his eyes to concentrate on the sounds Hamish's heart was making, then after a few seconds he leaned back on his heels and puffed his cheeks out in relief. 'Thank God, it's beginning to get a more normal beat. I think he's settling down now.' He turned round to see what was happening behind him. 'What the hell are we going to do about that ambulance?' he said. 'We've got to get Hamish to hospital pronto—he could still arrest and then we're in deep trouble.'

Terry bit her lip and looked at the men still struggling with the ambulance. 'We've no other option—we'll just have to take him in the Land Rover. If we clear the back, would the stretcher from the ambulance fit in?'

'Could do. Look, I'll go and do that with the lads. You stay with Hamish and monitor him.'

Atholl ran over to the small crowd of men still trying to hold the dogs at bay. They were having a difficult job and suddenly one of the dogs bolted through and tore straight for his stricken master, despite the shouts of the men. Terry sensed that the dog was bearing down on them but she wasn't about to leave Hamish. He needed to see her face and hear her talking to him, someone comforting to hang onto in the sea of pain he must be in.

The dog took no notice of Terry but skidded to a halt in the mud and licked Hamish's face, then dropped down by his side as if he were guarding him. That's all the animal wanted, thought Terry, to be near the man he loved.

'Leave him here,' she said firmly to a man who had raced over to try and move the dog. 'He's doing no harm, and, who knows, it may be of comfort to Hamish to know that his dog's near him.'

And after that they couldn't get the animal away from Hamish, although he seemed to sense that the people around his master were trying to help him, and didn't actively interfere when Hamish was lifted onto the stretcher and carried to Atholl's Land Rover. He growled ferociously when an attempt was made to shoo him off, but as long as he was allowed to trot by Hamish's side he was quite calm.

'We'll have to let Brandy come with us—the daft animal's not going to let us take Hamish away without him,' said Atholl. He looked up at one of the paramedics. 'Bill, you drive the vehicle and Terry and I will sit by Hamish and try and steady him. More haste, less speed is the byword and, for God's sake, don't go through any potholes.'

Crouched in the back of the Land Rover with a wet dog practically on her lap and the patient and Atholl crushed beside her on the other side was a scenario she couldn't possibly have envisaged when she'd left London a week or two ago, reflected Terry. She held Hamish's hand and squeezed it, trying to communicate to him that he was not alone, there were people caring for him. She smiled grimly to herself. No doubt about it—she'd been thrown in at the deep end!

She looked at Atholl, wet hair plastered like a seal's over his bent head as he concentrated on monitoring the man's heart, oblivious to everything else but keeping his patient stable. Occasionally he glanced out of the window to see how near the hospital they were, then nodded encouragingly at Terry as she tried her best to hold the stretcher steady over the rougher bits of road.

Hamish's eyes were open now, clouded with pain and fright. He moved his lips behind the oxygen mask, trying desperately to say something to his doctor. Atholl moved the mask slightly and leaned further forward to hear Hamish.

'Get my son to bring the sheep down from the top meadow,' the man whispered.

Atholl patted his hand. 'I will do, Hamish. Don't worry, you're doing fine.'

'Thank you,' whispered the man, closing his eyes, his face looking pinched and grey in the dim light of the vehicle.

After a journey that must have seemed an age to the stricken man, they deposited Hamish at the small hospital outside Scuola village. Atholl had telephoned ahead to warn them of the emergency admission and there was a team waiting to deal with Hamish as they arrived.

Atholl managed to slip a belt through the dog's collar and restrain the animal as his master was transferred to a trolley and pushed at speed to the resuscitation room. Both doctors watched as Hamish was taken away and Brandy whimpered as if aware that it would be some time before he saw Hamish again.

'It's going to be touch and go. Poor old Hamish...he's not out of the woods yet,' said Atholl wearily, bending to stroke the dog.

'You did your best—and at least you got him into sinus rhythm.'

Atholl shook his head and corrected her. 'It was a team effort, Terry. I couldn't have managed without you.'

For a second their eyes locked and a look of relief and triumph flickered between them. They grinned at each other, buoyed up by the adrenaline of success.

Then Atholl said briskly, 'Right, Bill can drive us back to his ambulance and tell Hamish's son to move the sheep. OK, Bill, let's go. I'll hold onto this dog until we've got there. Let's hope they've managed to extricate the ambulance—it's the only one we've got on the island.'

The two of them sat slumped in the steamy back of the vehicle, both feeling the sudden exhaustion that came with the anticlimax of dealing with a dramatic situation. The dog was lying across the edge of the seat, finally quiet as if he too was tired out.

Atholl's gazed drifted over to Terry, lying back with her eyes closed, her lashes sweeping her high cheekbones, wet hair plastered to her head and her mouth slightly open. He smiled to himself. She was as tough as any man—she'd just proved it!

CHAPTER FIVE

THE Land Rover bucked its way along the narrow twisting country road. Now that the patient had been delivered to the hospital, Bill seemed intent on getting back to the farm as quickly as possible, however rough the road was! Stretching his long legs out in front of him, Atholl massaged his shoulders to ease the tension of bending over Hamish for a prolonged time.

'God, that was touch and go,' he remarked. 'If we've saved him, it's been a great day's work.'

'Oh, I do hope so.' Terry brushed wet strands of hair out of her eyes and, despite the adrenaline that had been coursing round her body a few minutes ago, gave a huge yawn and leaned tiredly against the door. She felt depressed despite the fact that they'd helped to save a man's life. She was having one of those black moments when, out of the blue, something would trigger those ghastly memories. In her mind's eye she'd see a vivid picture of her father again, her last vision of him lying in her arms, his lips blue and his breath fading from his body.

The fact was that dealing with Hamish Stoddard had reminded her strongly of her father. He was the same age and the same build as her father had been, with similar thick white hair, and suddenly she felt very alone and far from anyone who cared for her.

She sighed, swallowing a lump in her throat and blinking back tears of self-pity, allowing her body to be jolted as Bill kept his foot on the accelerator as they rounded corners.

Atholl flicked a glance at her sad expression—the look that came over her from time to time. Losing her father had obviously been a terrible blow, but instinctively he felt there was something more to the story that she'd told him, something unresolved in her past, and he hated to see the heartbreak reflected in her eyes and drooping mouth.

'You all right?' he asked. 'Here, lean against me—not on that hard door. You'll be shaken to death. I may be a bit damp, but at least I'm not made of metal!'

He put an arm round Terry to pull her towards him and for a moment she hesitated, as if not quite sure about the offer, looking doubtfully up at his mud-streaked face and the rivulets of water that ran down from his soaked hair and onto his damp jersey that smelt of wet wool. Then the car accelerated over another pothole, jolting her sharply against the door again, and she smiled at him.

'Thanks. It is a bit uncomfortable here.'

She lay back against him, rather self-consciously at first but gradually succumbing to the broad comfort of his chest, and in the small steamy confines of the back of the Land Rover, where it was warm and intimate, the outside world began to recede. Terry forgot about Bill driving the vehicle, or the dog panting by Atholl's side, even the aching sadness of missing her father. All she was aware of was just how close Atholl was to her. She relaxed gratefully against his broad frame with the comforting damp warmth and rough feel of his thick jersey around her, his breath on her cheek.

Did he feel the gradual heightening of the atmosphere too, Terry wondered, or was it just her over-active sensitivity when she was feeling rather down and leaning against a man who oozed sex appeal? She closed her eyes, savouring the comfort of his arm supporting her, feeling her sadness slip away. When she opened them again he was looking down at her intently, then the blue of his eyes darkened and he tightened his grip round her, twisting his body so that she was pulled against his chest.

'You looked rather miserable a minute ago,' he said huskily. 'Is anything wrong?'

To Terry's embarrassment two large tears rolled down her cheeks and she gave an involuntary sob. That was what happened when people were kind to you and you felt very low—your defences came down and your emotions got the better of you. She gulped and swallowed back the large lump that had settled in her throat.

'Sorry, it's nothing really. I don't know what came over me. It was just that I was reminded of something...'

'Yes?' he said gently, bending his head nearer hers so that he could hear her above the noise of the Land Rover. 'Tell me, Terry, what's troubling you?'

She shook her head mutely. Her background had to remain a secret and, however kind Atholl's enquiry, the baggage from her past life was a closed door as far as he—or anyone else—was concerned. It was unlikely that she could ever reveal the whole reason for her flight to Scotland.

'I miss my father very much,' she said at last. 'It comes over me in waves—but I'll be all right. I'm being silly.' She gave a watery smile and brushed the tears roughly away from her eyes.

'You must also be missing your friends and London—your social life,' he suggested.

She pulled away from him abruptly. 'I'll get over it,' she said sharply. 'I've left all that behind.'

Atholl looked quizzically at her. Just what had she left behind? She seemed unwilling to expand on any aspect of her life in London. He stroked away a stray tear on her cheek with his finger and turned her head towards him.

'No pangs, then, for the bright lights?'

The look in his warm blue eyes was compassionate, as if he knew what she was going through, and again she felt those treacherous tears well up in her eyes. Angrily she tried to blink them back. What a mawkish idiot she was being. Atholl squeezed her to him comfortingly, then after a second's pause lowered his head to hers and brushed her forehead with his lips, a feather-light kiss that sent a scorching flood of heat through her body. It was so brief a touch that at first she wondered if he'd actually kissed her. She looked up at him questioningly and then it seemed only natural for her arms to wind round his neck, bringing him nearer, and he kissed her again, this time full on her lips, and his firm mouth felt sweet, salty and demanding.

Oh, how she'd needed this sort of closeness and comfort again, to feel that someone cared for her, was even interested in her... Giddily she wondered at the back of her mind if wasn't rather dangerous to be kissing a colleague like this when she wasn't interested in men—especially a man she hardly knew. Everything seemed to be happening so quickly. A thousand butterflies were fluttering inside her and her heart was doing a mad tattoo against her ribs. Why, only a few months ago she had thought she was madly in love with Max, and only he could ever light her fire. How odd that suddenly every nerve in her body was tingling with anticipation and longing to do more than just kiss a man who was practically a stranger!

As his warm lips sought her cool ones, her lively imagination leapt further ahead. What would it be like to make love to him properly? To feel his hands caressing her, to lose herself in everything but the delight of his touch?

Then all of a sudden she felt Atholl pulling away from her and gently disengaging her arms from around him. Embarrassment made her cheeks redden, and she tried not to look too startled.

He shook his head with a wry smile and said in a joking manner, 'I'm sorry about that...a bit of an overreaction after a tough afternoon. I just hated to see you upset and, well, I...I just wanted to thank you for your help, show you how grateful I am. I didn't mean to overstep the mark!' He grinned at her. 'But we worked so well together, didn't we? It's great to know that we have a good working relationship.'

A good working relationship? It had seemed to Terry for a moment there that it had gone way beyond a 'working relationship', but she'd obviously misinterpreted it—he was making it very clear that that was what he wanted. It had been nothing more than an over-enthusiastic hug to comfort her.

'It was just part of my job—as you said, a team effort,' she said lightly, and chuckled as if being kissed by the most stunning-looking man she'd been near for some time was just a normal occurrence, the usual way one thanked a colleague and of no consequence whatsoever.

But inwardly she felt the acute embarrassment of taking far too much for granted, and it left her slightly deflated. It had obviously been just an honest and kindly gesture on his part to comfort someone who had started blubbing without apparent reason, and she had read more into the situation than Atholl had meant.

She drew back shakily from the warmth of his body. His mouth had felt so sweet on hers, so right, so comforting, and she had responded far too passionately to the light kisses he'd given her. He probably assumed, she thought gloomily, that she wasn't averse to a casual encounter, an easy bit of sex on the side.

She smiled brightly and said briskly, 'So, when we've deposited Bill, it's back to the surgery?'

'Afraid so. It's the mother-and-baby clinic this afternoon—do you think you could take that with Sue? I've got a meeting with that wretched man from the health authority.' Atholl's voice was casual, relaxed, as if kissing her hadn't raised his heartbeat at all. And as if to emphasise that, he shouted out over the noise of the engine to Bill, 'Could you tell Hamish's son about the sheep Bill? Terry and I have to get back.'

Terry had almost forgotten about Bill driving the vehicle, and looked at him with some embarrassment. Had he seen Atholl and her locked in a close embrace in the back? It wouldn't appear so as he and Atholl started up a mundane conversation about the weather and the difficulty of ever getting the ambulance out of the mud, without a hint of self-consciousness. Indeed, Atholl seemed to have forgotten all about her, bending his head to look at the dog and stroking him gently.

Atholl tried to breathe deeply and slowly, endeavouring to calm himself. Why the hell had he just kissed Terry like that—given in to the powerful attraction he suddenly admitted he'd felt ever since he'd first seen her on the quayside less than two weeks ago? She'd looked so uncomfortable and rather vulnerable, sitting squashed in the back of the Land Rover with him, and that was why he'd invited her to lean against him. But once he'd felt that soft body next to his some madness had overcome him and he'd felt an irresistible urge to kiss her, try and comfort her. If he wasn't careful he'd be in too deep with a woman he knew next to nothing about, and who, for all he knew, could cause him as much aggravation as Zara Grahame had.

For a second an image of his forthright mother came into his mind—he could almost hear her scornful words. 'Atholl Brodie, you never learn, do you? I told you to keep away from those high-falutin' girls who've been brought up in gilded cages. You want to stick to your own sort—a girl from your own background and area. You're a fool to try and fit in where you don't belong!'

He flicked a look at Terry. She was looking out of the window, her delectable profile turned slightly away from him, tip-tilted nose, lips slightly parted, and he groaned inwardly. They had had very different upbringings. He guessed from her speech and manner that she had a background of wealth and privilege, but the truth was that now he knew how it felt to kiss Terry, he couldn't wait to do it again—and plunge his life into turmoil once more, he thought savagely to himself.

A day or two later Atholl came into Terry's room to remind her that they were doing a home visit to the Mackie sisters who lived in one of the cottages perched high on the hillside on one of the remote estates on the island.

'It's a good opportunity to show you a bit of the island so that you have some idea of the layout when you come to do your own home visits,' he said.

There was something about his brisk, businesslike manner, with no hint of intimacy, that gave Terry the impression that he wanted to maintain a distance between them after the episode in the Land Rover. He'd also made a point of staying out of the house until she was in bed. And that was absolutely for the best, she thought resolutely, picking up her medical bag and slinging a coat round her shoulders.

Yet again the weather had changed and now the skies were turning blue and the sun was warm on their faces as they got into the car. Shona was sitting in the back, her ears pricked excitedly for the outing, wagging her tail in anticipation of a long walk. But the easy camaraderie of the other day seemed to have vanished and silence hung heavily between them on the journey. Terry very aware that Atholl felt they had become too intimate that day. She tried hard to dredge up some small talk to lighten the atmosphere as they arrived at the sisters' home—one half of a pair of cottages with a pretty little garden to the side and back.

'It's like Hansel and Gretel's cottage,' she remarked brightly. 'A sweet little place.'

'It's part of the Dunsford Estate,' explained Atholl, seeming to relax a little. 'Kate and Sarah's father was the old laird's gamekeeper, or "stalker" as he liked to be called. When he died they continued living here and helping at the big house, cooking and cleaning. Now they're both in their eighties and very independent—it'll be hard to get them to accept help.'

He knocked at the door and they waited for a few moments. He knocked again but there was still no reply, so he tried to turn the doorhandle, but it was locked.

'Funny,' he muttered. 'They aren't very mobile, but they usually sit in the room just behind this door. I would've expected them to answer it more quickly than this—and I've never known them lock the door.' He tried to peer through the lace curtains of the small window by the door, then gave an impatient exclamation. 'I'll go round the back and look in through the windows—you wait here in case they do answer the door.'

Just then a quavery voice sounded behind them. 'Hello, Doctor! We didn't think you'd be here so quickly! We've just been scrubbing up a few early potatoes!'

Two frail figures were making their way towards Atholl and Terry from the garden path that led from a small vegetable patch, both dressed in similar dark coats with felt hats on their heads. One of the old ladies was coughing and wheezing and the other one supported her.

'That's quite a heavy bag you've got there, Kate,' said Atholl, striding forward, taking the potatoes from her and putting one hand under the arm of her sister. 'Have you got the key of the house ready?'

'Aye—it's somewhere in my pocket.' Kate fumbled for it then handed it to Atholl. 'We don't normally lock the door, as you know…but something bad has happened, hasn't it, Sarah?'

The other sister looked up at both the doctors and they noticed she was trembling. 'We've been burgled, Doctor,' she quavered. 'We were down the garden after Sue, your community nurse, had left this morning. When we came back there was a terrible mess…' She stopped and looked helplessly at Kate. 'I…I don't like to think about it…'

It was obvious they'd both had a terrible shock. Atholl looked grim. 'Come in now, Kate, and, Sarah—sit you down, both of you. We'll put the kettle on and you must tell us what happened over a cup of tea.'

His voice was kind and compassionate, but Terry could see

the steely anger behind his words. How could anyone steal from these two vulnerable little women who had worked hard all their lives? They all went into the house and the two doctors stared in silent dismay at the overturned chairs, the contents of a small desk thrown over the floor, a cup and saucer that had been knocked off a table and lay smashed on the tiled fireplace.

'We…we couldn't bear to sit in the house,' said Kate. 'That's why we were in the garden.'

'I'm ringing the police,' declared Atholl. 'I want them to come and see this before we tidy it up—there may be finger-prints. But first I want you both to sit on the sofa…'

'And I'll get some nice hot tea,' suggested Terry.

'Ah, I'd better introduce you,' said Atholl, drawing Terry forward. 'This is my new colleague in the practice, Dr Terry Younger. I thought it would be nice if you could meet her and she meet you—I'm sorry it wasn't in happier circumstances.'

Both old ladies smiled tremulously at her. 'It's nice to meet you, Doctor,' quavered Kate. 'It'll be nice for Dr Atholl to have some help, won't it, Sarah, while old Dr Euan recovers?'

While Atholl rang the police on his mobile, Terry served the shocked sisters with sweet tea which they sipped grate-fully, the warm liquid and the mere fact of being looked after, helping them to relax.

'Do you know what's been taken?' she asked gently.

'Just a few wee bits of jewellery that belonged to our mother—we don't think it's worth much.' Kate dabbed her eyes and sighed. 'Of course, it meant a lot to us.' Then her expres-sion changed and she drew herself up to her full small height on the sofa and looked belligerently up at Terry. 'If they catch whoever did this I'll give them a piece of my mind—that I will!'

Terry smiled at the feisty little woman. It was good that she was feeling angry and not too broken by the nasty episode. The more she and her sister could talk about it, the better they would feel, and if not come to terms with the situation at least learn to live with it.

'That's right, Kate, you must feel absolutely furious about all of this, but when the police have come we'll tidy it up and make sure everything's secure.'

Atholl came back into the room—his tall figure in the small space seemed a reassuring presence in the wreckage of their little parlour. Something about his stature and calm manner made things seem more normal, safer, despite the abnormality of the situation. The old ladies looked up at him hopefully, as if he could put their broken world back in order.

'The police are on their way now,' he informed them. He sat down by the old ladies and took Sarah's hand. She seemed the more shocked of the two, gazing sadly ahead of her. 'Now, Sarah, don't worry, we'll get to the bottom of this.'

Sarah focussed on him and said in a bewildered way. 'I don't know who could have done it—there's no one around here who would dream of it. Our next-door neighbours and the farmers nearby are friends that we've known for many years and no one else comes up here.'

It was a good point. They were in a remote part of the island and only locals would know that two vulnerable old ladies lived in the cottage. Apart from a few walkers, nobody generally strayed this far up the hill.

She plucked nervously at her collar. 'I…I don't feel safe here any more. Suppose they come back?'

Atholl patted her hand. 'Now, I've had a good idea—how would you like Shona to stay with you for a few nights? She wouldn't let anyone harm you, and perhaps you'd feel safer if she was around?'

For the first time Sarah looked a little brighter. 'Would Shona not mind coming here?'

Atholl laughed. 'She'd love it—doesn't she always get biscuits here which I never allow her at home? She's in the car now—I'll bring her in and she can have tea with us!'

It was obvious that Shona acted as a huge tonic to Kate and Sarah, for they became quite animated and insisted on going into the little kitchen and bringing out a whole box of biscuits.

'Shona was actually born in this cottage,' Atholl explained quietly to Terry as Shona bounded in, wagging her tail delightedly at the prospect of being spoilt, going over to the old ladies and pushing her nose onto their laps. 'She was one of a litter that Kate and Sarah's old dog had four years ago. Sadly Polly died not long after that, but Shona looks remarkably like her.'

'It's a wonderful idea.' Terry smiled. 'They've really cheered up and it's given them something else to think about.'

Both doctors watched in amusement as the sisters fussed over Shona and found Polly's old basket for her to sleep in. But Terry noted how badly the old ladies walked and the difficulty they had getting up from their chairs.

'They look very unsteady,' she murmured to Atholl. 'What are the chances of them slipping in the bathroom—or anywhere else, for that matter?'

Atholl nodded, and while they waited for the police to arrive he broached the subject gently of someone coming in daily to give them a hand. They both shook their heads vehemently, protesting that they could look after each other.

'We don't need or want anyone fussing over us every day—we're fine as we are,' said Kate stoutly.

'Why don't you at least consider wearing an alarm disc round your neck?' suggested Terry. 'You are very isolated here and if you're in trouble of any kind—from falling to being worried about prowlers—you press the disc and that goes through to a central monitoring system that will send help if they can't get hold of you over the monitor in the house.'

'Ah, but we could easily press it by mistake, and we'd be very embarrassed,' protested Kate.

'No problem. You just tell the person who contacts you a few moments after the disc has been pressed that it was done in error, and no one will come. Several of my patients in London had it, and on at least two occasions it saved their lives. No one disturbs you unless you need help.'

Both sisters looked at each other questioningly, seeking the other's approval before agreeing to anything.

'It really would be a good idea, you know,' persuaded Atholl gently. 'It would stop all of us worrying—and, of course, Sue would still come and see you on a regular basis to check your general health.'

'Well, perhaps,' said Sarah slowly. 'Now we've had this nasty business it could be reassuring to know that we can call on someone easily—if we weren't near the phone and we needed help urgently, that is. Would you be able to organise that?'

'Of course,' said Atholl, shooting a relieved glance at Terry. 'I think it would be a wise move.'

After the police had been and gone, Atholl and Terry quickly put the scattered things back into place. Kate showed them an old photograph she had of her mother wearing a piece of the jewellery that had been stolen—a pretty little Victorian necklace.

'I don't suppose we'll ever see it again—but at least we're

both OK, and that's all that matters,' she said. 'And we'd like to thank you doctors for all your help, wouldn't we, Sarah?'

'No trouble at all,' said Atholl. 'Now, I'll go and get Shona's lead from the car, and an old bone she likes to play with.'

He went out and Sarah put a restraining hand on Terry's arm, holding her back for a second. 'It's good to see young Dr Atholl has some reliable help now—he's been through such a bad time with that Dr Grahame.' She put a hand to her mouth guiltily. 'Oh, dear, perhaps I shouldn't be saying that— but maybe you'll be just the girl to cheer him up!' Her eyes twinkled and she turned to her sister. 'He needs a bit of fun in his life, doesn't he, Kate?'

Kate nodded gravely. 'Aye, he's a good man who's had a rough time. We'd all love to see him settled happily. We've known him since he was a little boy and used to come for the holidays with his uncle.'

'I suppose he feels almost like one of your family,' re- marked Terry, longing to know just what the story was about this Dr Grahame and how she'd affected Atholl's life so much. To ask him outright would seem too intrusive, she reflected, but surely she could find out from Bunty? She determined to do that when the moment seemed right.

'It's a very odd thing about that burglary,' Atholl said as they drove back to The Sycamores. 'There really aren't many people walking or even living near the Mackie sisters. A few campers in the middle of summer perhaps, but I know there's no one at the site at the moment.' His jaw tightened. 'I just hope they pick up whoever's burgled those old ladies.'

'They're very fond of you,' said Terry. 'They said they'd known you for many years.'

'That's true—I remember them plying me with sweeties

when I went with my uncle on a visit sometimes. In a place like this there's often a long-standing relationship with your GP.'

They were back at The Sycamores and Terry got out of the car. 'I'll see you tomorrow, then. I know you're off to see your uncle again now and I'll be in bed by the time you get back. I hope he's doing well.'

He smiled at her and said quietly, 'Thanks…and thank you again for your help today.'

There was sudden self-consciousness between them, as if they had both remembered at the same second that intimate interlude a day or two ago in the back of the Land Rover. Their eyes locked and in Terry's mind she felt again the soft touch of his lips on hers, the thudding of his heart when she'd leant against him, the scratch of late-day stubble on his chin. It might have meant nothing to him, she thought wryly as she ran up the steps of the surgery, but it had been a moment of bliss that she wouldn't forget in a hurry.

She bit her lip and looked back at him for a second before she opened the surgery door. How stupid she was being— surely the last few months had taught her that men were not to be trusted. Max had destroyed her happy life, and it would surely never be the same again.

Atholl watched as she disappeared, looking deliciously feminine in her neat skirt and pale blue silk blouse. She probably thought he'd been a chancy character trying it on with her the other day, although she'd been decent enough to make light of it. He sighed. The moment that he'd kissed her should never have happened, but a sudden impulse that had driven him on to throw caution to the winds—and now he couldn't stop thinking about her.

Atholl revved up the engine, turning the car round in a tight circle in the drive, and started out towards the ferry, trying to make sense of his mixed emotions. He parked the car in the car park, and sat for a minute staring out at the sparkling sea. For some time now he'd been treading on eggshells where women had been concerned—he'd been bruised and humiliated by one woman and he was damned if he was going to take the chance of any other female doing the same to him.

An image of Terry's sweet face came into his mind and he sighed. She had lit more than a little spark of attraction in him—but she was essentially a city girl like Zara and she was only going to be here for a short time. No good thinking they could form any permanent relationship—it would just be a rerun of the scenario with Zara.

He got out of the car and looked towards the little ferry sailing across the sound and shrugged. He would look forward to spending a whole day with Terry when they went to help at the outward bound course. She would be a pleasant companion and it would be fun to show her the beautiful countryside, without getting too involved. And perhaps he'd find out more about this beautiful woman with the background she kept so close to her chest.

CHAPTER SIX

THE Sunday they were scheduled to go to the outward bound centre dawned bright and clear. Atholl banged loudly on Terry's bedroom door.

'Time to get up,' he called. He got a muffled grunt in response, so he banged again. 'Come on, Terry, no time to lose!'

Still no response, so he opened the door and peered round. 'Wake up!' he bellowed. 'The weather forecast's good for this morning but dicey later on, so we need to get a move on or the abseiling might be off.'

Terry stirred slightly then relaxed again, lying curled up on her side with one hand supporting her head, long lashes sweeping the curve of her flushed cheek. There was something so vulnerable about her, her lips slightly parted as if just waiting to be kissed. Atholl felt a moment's shame as he looked at her. He shouldn't be here in this room without her knowledge—it was as if he were taking advantage of her somehow—but he did have to wake her, didn't he? He was holding a mug of tea in one hand and with the other he reached down and tickled her nose.

She stirred again and brushed his hand away. She'd just been enjoying a wonderful dream where she and Atholl had been swimming in one of the little coves on the island. The sea was rather rough and the waves kept tossing her into his arms as they were swept towards the shore. His body was wet and slippery against hers and he held her tight to him so that she wouldn't be submerged by the next wave. She could feel every muscle in his taut body, his legs firm against hers, bracing her against the swell of the sea. He was laughing down at her, white teeth in a tanned face...then suddenly a little feather landed on her nose and started to tickle it. Impatiently she tried to brush it away, longing to get to the next stage of her dream, but it continued to irritate her.

She opened her eyes in exasperation and sat up suddenly in bed, looking slightly bewildered when Atholl's familiar face only a foot away from her swam into view. She clutched the sheets against her when she realised that she was no longer dreaming but the subject of her dream was looking down at her!

'What the...? What's happened? What are you doing here?'

Atholl's gaze took in her flushed cheeks, dishevelled hair and a flash of soft creamy breasts as she tried to maintain her modesty, and felt his heartbeat accelerate as if a button had been pressed. What wouldn't he give to tear off his clothes and leap into the warm bed with her and to hell with going over for the day with the outward bound group! He was beginning to realise that having Terry living in the same house as him could be one big temptation.

'Wake up, sleepyhead,' he said huskily. 'Sorry to disturb you, but we ought to get going if we're to get to the outward bound group before they set off.'

Terry's eyes widened. 'Oh, I'd forgotten all about that. I was so exhausted after the past few days...'

He grinned. 'Exhausted? It's just a normal everyday story

of country doctors, reviving someone with a heart attack in a rainstorm, helping two old ladies who'd been burgled....'

She laughed. 'So I'm beginning to realise! But I'd been dreaming, you see.'

'Not a nightmare, I hope?'

A warm flush suffused Terry's cheeks as she recalled just what the subject of her dream had been. 'No,' she murmured. 'Definitely not a nightmare.'

He stood looking at her with twinkling eyes as if he could read her mind and was amused by it. She waited for a moment, slightly embarrassed, expecting him to leave.

'I'll be down soon,' she hinted. 'It won't take me long.'

'Sorry—didn't mean to intrude. I thought you'd like a cup of tea, or rather a mug,' he added with a grin. 'I don't do cups!'

He held out a mug and she leant forward to take it, but in trying not to let the sheet fall down and expose the skimpy baby doll she wore in bed, she fumbled it and the mug clattered to the floor, spilling the tea over the sheets.

'Oh, no! What am I like?'

She bent over the bed to retrieve the mug at the same time as Atholl bent down to pick it up. Their heads almost collided and they both froze in mid-action, their faces inches apart.

'Sorry!' they exclaimed in unison, then stopped and gazed at each other, a crackle of attraction between them springing into life like a current between magnets.

How close they were. Terry could see the black flecks in his blue sexy eyes, the black lashes fringing them, and smell the just-washed soapy clean, male smell of him. It was almost as if her dream was continuing. All her senses screamed out to lean towards him and feel once more those firm sexy lips on hers, his hand caressing her body. Somewhere in the back of her mind a hundred warning thoughts whirred round. Was she going to embarrass them both as she had done last time? He'd no doubt think she was up for sex at any opportunity! Even more to the point, once they'd started kissing in such a setting as this bedroom, for God's sake, where would it end?

'There's still some tea left in the mug,' Atholl said gruffly. 'Why don't you drink it now?'

Terry pushed herself back properly into the bed and pulled the sheet up to her chin. 'Er...I'll have it in a minute, thank you,' she said breathlessly, aware that he was looking down at her, an unreadable expression in his blue eyes.

He put the mug on the bedside table carefully and sat down on the bed, taking out a handkerchief to mop up some of the spilt liquid on the sheets and over her arms.

'The tea didn't scald you, did it?' he asked.

'No...not at all.'

Terry's voice came out in a husky little croak, her pulse speeding up slightly at his proximity and the thought that if she wanted to she could throw off her sheet and pull him alongside her with no trouble at all! She couldn't help but give a nervous giggle at the thought, turning it unsuccessfully into a cough.

He smiled at her. 'Right. Well, I'd better go and get breakfast started,' he said, not moving, his gaze travelling slowly over her face.

Terry licked her lips nervously, aware of his close proximity to her, half hoping he'd move and yet longing for him not to.

'You...you've still got quite a scar from the accident,' she said at last, to break the tension between them. Her hand went out to touch the cut he'd sustained on his chin trying to get Maisie out of the car on the day Terry had arrived.

'And you've got a piece of hair across your eye,' he

murmured, leaning over her and removing a wisp of hair from her forehead. His hand stayed on her cheek for a moment, then strayed across to her ear before he took it back. She froze for a second, a mixture of excited anticipation and apprehension flickering through her body.

'Funny how long we seem to have known each other,' he murmured.

Terry's voice caught in her throat. 'Only a few weeks actually…'

He smiled. 'True, but I want to know more about you. Was losing your father the only thing that brought you to Scuola? You've only given me sketchy details…'

His piercing blue eyes looked intently into hers as if he could decipher just what had happened to make her leave London. He watched her eyes slide away from his and he was sure that she was withholding something. Suddenly he was determined to find out more, to crack the mysterious code that was Terry's past.

She answered pugnaciously, 'I told you before—I wanted a change. My father's death precipitated that. I don't need to elaborate. Anyway, is it relevant to our situation?'

Terry turned her face away from that searching look, determined not to divulge any more, but he took her chin in his hand and gently turned it back so that she had to face him.

'I've got to know what makes you tick,' he said gently. 'Don't you see that if we're to work well together we have to be friends? Friends usually know each other's backgrounds, don't they? I'm making a shrewd guess here, Terry. I've a feeling that it was a broken love affair that first made you think of leaving London, before your father died.'

He watched the stricken look in her eyes and felt he'd hit

on something like the truth. Terry was silent. She couldn't tell him everything, but she felt that perhaps he did deserve to know a little about her background.

'That was part of it,' she admitted at last. 'The truth is, I fell for my ex, Max, because I thought he was everything I wanted—charming, charismatic, good fun, good looks...' She gave a mirthless laugh. 'And he could give a girl a good time!'

'Sounds as if he ticked a lot of boxes,' remarked Atholl drily, his clear eyes never leaving her.

'Oh, yes, on the surface it looked good.' A bitter tone entered her voice. 'Underneath he was a devious and selfish opportunist, and he did things that had, well, wide-ranging consequences. It taught me the lesson never to let my heart rule my head. That's basically it, Atholl. It was enough to make me want to leave the area.'

There was no need for her to go into any more details. The rest of her story was one she couldn't divulge—that had to remain a secret. Then, as if pushing that thought to the back of her mind, she said lightly, 'Let's stop talking about me— what about you? What happened between you and my attractive predecessor, Dr Grahame, I keep hearing about?'

A startled expression crossed Atholl's face, as if he hadn't anticipated Terry asking him such a blunt question. He stood up and walked over to the window, looking out at the fields beyond and bunching his fists tensely in his pockets, before turning back to her with a wry grin.

'Tit for tat, eh? It seems we've had similar experiences— although in my case much of the blame was mine. But it's a long story, rather boring really.'

Boring? Not to Terry, fascinated and intrigued to know more about the background of this sexy, good-looking man.

'Please go on,' she said. 'I...I'd be really interested to know what happened.'

He shrugged. 'To put it briefly, Zara was a liar—she strung me along. She deceived me, and deception is an act of betrayal in my eyes.' His eyes became flint hard. 'And God help anyone who tries to deceive me again.'

Terry felt a shiver of worry go through her. How would he react if he knew that she wasn't the person he thought she was? That she was a sham, someone built on a tissue of lies, a woman whose background had had to be obliterated?

'Wh-what did she lie about?'

He gave a mirthless laugh. 'I don't think you'd believe me if I told you. I was so incredibly naive—idiotic actually.'

Terry sat up, hugging her arms around her. 'Why shouldn't I believe you? Come on—tell me what she did.'

Atholl sighed and suddenly looked a little older and tireder. 'We met at medical school. She was very attractive, one of those girls who seemed to have everything—good looks, good fun, full of confidence.'

Terry felt a sudden surge of jealousy over this paragon of attraction. 'You fell for each other, then?'

'I should've known better. She and I came from completely different backgrounds. Her family were wealthy, rubbed shoulders with privileged people. I was from the Glasgow Gorbals and that was a very different world.'

'But you were just as good as she was—why should that make any difference?'

'Because we saw things differently. I was used to scraping together every penny I could—Zara didn't have those worries. But then when we started working as junior doctors there wasn't much time to spend money anyway, and the differences between us weren't so noticeable.'

'And so...what happened then?'

Atholl sat on the windowsill, leaning back against the window, a remote expression on his face. 'We became engaged.'

'So you loved her,' stated Terry rather flatly. Somehow it seemed that there was a lot hanging on this question.

There was a short silence and Terry watched his face turn to one of bitterness. 'I thought I did,' he said at last. 'She was attractive, the centre of attention. I suppose I was flattered when she made it plain she fancied me.'

'And were you happy?'

He shrugged. 'Life was fun when we could manage time off together. Zara loved nightclubs, partying, shopping...it was a hectic social whirl and I didn't realise that actually deep down I didn't terribly like doing those things. But she was a city girl through and through. I know now that we were totally incompatible.'

'But you had come from a city too,' pointed out Terry. 'Surely there must have been some understanding between you?'

He nodded. 'Possibly—but then my uncle began having health problems and offered me a job on Scuola, a place I loved from coming here as a child. It was going to be a temporary arrangement so Zara was happy to come here and join the practice for a while. But Uncle Euan decided to cut back on his hours even more and it became plain that he would never come back full time.'

'So you wanted to stay and Zara didn't?' suggested Terry.

'She began to hate it here. We'd set a date for the wedding—just a small affair, although, of course, it was of great interest to everyone on Scuola—local GP in love match sort of thing,' he said drily. 'Zara was quite pleased to be married here in the pretty little church down the road. A television company was doing a film about the area and our wedding was going to be featured in it—that appealed to her.'

'So…so you got married then?'

Atholl shook his head and his voice was unemotional, detached. 'Two days before the wedding I came back to the flat we were sharing rather earlier than usual. I found Zara in bed with one of her brother's friends—a guest at the wedding.'

Terry stared at him in horror. 'You found her…just before the wedding day?'

'Thank God it wasn't after the wedding,' Atholl remarked lightly. 'She made a fool of me, deceived me, and it hurt. I won't pretend it didn't, even if I'd realised deep down that we weren't meant for each other. I won't make that mistake again.'

Terry was silent for a moment, then she said softly, 'Wow, what an awful story, Atholl. I reckon you had a lucky escape, then.'

No wonder Atholl was so happy to be single! She looked at his dark, sexy eyes and the hard-boned structure of his good-looking face. It was no surprise that Isobel was nervous that he was prey to any female who joined the practice—she didn't want him to run the risk of being hurt again.

Terry looked away, a little chill of worry flickering through her mind. What he would say if he knew her whole story? Then she reasoned that she hadn't deceived him all that much about herself—just a few little white lies. And at least she'd told him about Max—or at least some of the story about Max.

'So now we have no secrets between us,' said Atholl with a grin. 'We're open books to each other!'

'You only know a little about me,' she parried nervously.

He laughed. 'Don't be so mysterious. I know enough about you to see how uncomplicated you are. You're a great doctor, I like and trust you,' he said with emphasis. 'And something else,' he murmured slowly, touching her face and looking down at her intently, 'You're very, very…'

Then an unreadable expression crossed his face and he checked himself, his voice trailing away as if he was about to say too much, reveal more of his thoughts than he should. He stood up abruptly, shooting a look at his watch.

'Hell—it's nine o'clock!' he exclaimed, raking a hand through his hair and striding to the door. 'I forgot our date with Pete and the boys at The Culleens. Let's get going!'

Terry stared after him as he thundered down the little stairs, and sighed, a mixture of thoughts racing through her mind. She'd been certain for a second that Atholl had been going to say something rather complimentary to her then—but it was clear that after his experience he was loath to speak those thoughts aloud. At least he'd said he liked her, even if Zara Grahame had made him as wary of commitment as putting his hand in a fire.

The little party of people strode away from The Culleens towards the outcrop of rocks at the base of the hills, leaving behind the loch and a buzzard lazily circling above it. The sun was shining brightly and it was quite warm. All around them was the low murmur of bees and somewhere high above a lark was singing its heart out over the sweep of moorland before them.

Terry glanced across at Atholl, his rangy figure dressed in old shorts revealing strong muscular legs, his powerful body carrying a huge rucksack as if it were no more than a bag of cotton wool. A mixture of happiness and apprehension flick-

ered through her. This was the guy who'd made it fairly clear
only an hour ago that he thought quite well of her—but he'd
also made it clear that he regarded anything less than the truth
as an act of betrayal. How would he react if he ever learned
that she was not the person she claimed to be?

She shifted her rucksack to a more comfortable position
on her back and shook herself mentally, forcing her worries
to the back of her mind. Whatever happened, today she was
going to live for the moment and enjoy this lovely day as
much as she could!

She, Atholl and Pete walked briskly together behind the
four strapping young men.

'This is all so beautiful,' she breathed. 'I can hardly believe
it's real!'

Atholl turned his face and winked at her, then held her eyes
in his for a second too long for comfort. 'It's certainly a place
of natural beauty—don't you agree, Pete?' he said teasingly.

Terry made a face back at him then quickly changed the
subject, saying brightly, 'Is Sally OK? It's only a week or so
to go now before the baby comes, isn't it?'

Pete patted his mobile. 'She promised she'd let me know
when she feels the first twinge—in fact, she's gone into
Scuola village today to see a friend, so I do feel a little more
relaxed about things. At least she's near the hospital and I can
concentrate on the boys here.'

'Did you tackle Zac about taking cannabis?' asked Atholl.

An expression of exasperation passed Pete's face. 'Yup, he
did actually admit to having a few spliffs, almost as if he
wanted to see how far he could go. Sally and I were mortified that he'd managed to hide the stuff and I threw the book
at him. One more strike and he's out.'

'And how did he take that?'

'He looked relieved, as if he'd expected to be sent back to Glasgow. He promised he'd tread the straight and narrow.' Pete smiled wryly. 'I just hope he can stick to it.'

Atholl turned to Terry. 'He's the one with the most troubled background. He has a disabled mother who was virtually abandoned by Zac's father, although the man keeps coming back and abusing them both when he wants a roof over his head. But I know Zac does like it here—enough to make him try and keep clean.'

'What about the others?' enquired Terry. 'They've settled OK?'

'Oh, sure,' said Pete. 'They've even become part of the community in a small way. They were all helping to dig and tidy up some of the older people's gardens the other day!'

Pete stopped walking and pointed to a high outcrop of rock on the other side of the river running beside them.

'Here we are. We can go over the bridge here and walk up the hill to the side of the rock to the top and then do some abseiling before we have lunch.'

Terry swallowed and looked up at the steep drop. It looked horribly high and suddenly she didn't seem quite as hungry as she had been earlier! She felt Atholl's amused, perceptive eyes on her and stuck her chin out in determination. She wasn't going to give anyone the chance to say she'd wimped out!

'I can't wait.' She smiled.

From the top it looked even more of a sheer drop. The sheep grazing on the moors below seemed like toys. Atholl put on a helmet and began to buckle on his harness and Pete clipped the safety rope to it before Atholl began to descend.

Terry's eyes flicked over his athletic body as he leant back against the rope, confident and relaxed, and her heart did a quick flip when she thought of that same body pressed against hers in his vehicle the other day. She bit her lip. Delightful though it was to let her thoughts stray to Atholl, she had to stop thinking of the man so much. She was here to assist, not moon about like a lovesick teenager! She made herself concentrate on what Pete was saying, hoping some of the information would rub off on her.

'Now, boys,' instructed Pete, 'watch what Atholl does— how he braces himself against the rock with his feet, keeping his legs straight. He's leaning back and feeding the rope through his hands in a controlled manner. The braking device on his harness won't let him slip.'

It seemed to Terry that Atholl took about two minutes to almost float down, although she was sure it would seem a lot longer than that when she did it!

Zac was chosen to go next, and he seemed very enthusiastic, stuffing his shaven head into a helmet and eagerly scrambling over the drop.

'Not too fast,' warned Pete. 'Take it slowly. Once you've got experience you can go more quickly.'

Zac grinned around at the others. 'Knowing how to do this could come in handy if I have to make a quick getaway,' he remarked cheekily, and winked at Terry.

She laughed. There was something of the lovable rogue about Zac. 'Be careful what you say, Zac…' she smilingly remarked.

Pete murmured wryly to her, 'Unfortunately, what he says has a kernel of truth in it—some people say this sort of activity holiday just makes these lads fitter to do more crime!'

At last it was Terry's turn and she forced herself to look

excited and enthusiastic as she peered over the edge to the small figures below, looking up at her.

'You'll be fine,' said Pete encouragingly, as if he could read the panic raging through her.

She swallowed hard and somehow managed to lower herself gingerly from the top, her face perilously near the rock face as she started to descend inch by cautious inch.

'Keep moving,' called Pete. 'You're doing really well! Don't look down!'

Terry imagined several pairs of eyes, including Atholl's, glued to her as she descended, and gritted her teeth, forcing herself to keep calm and not freeze. Fleetingly she thought of the predictable working life she'd led in London when the most nerve-racking thing that had happened had been a man appearing with a knife at the health centre one evening. Somehow this seemed much more daunting. Then gradually she began to get the hang of it, finding a kind of rhythm as she paid out the rope, and a feeling of exhilaration swept through her as she relaxed against the harness and allowed her legs to guide her down the cliff face.

'This is fun!' she yelled as she swung down, and in no time at all her feet touched the ground. There was a feeling of achievement and satisfaction, and from doing it herself she realised just how much these under-privileged boys would get out of it—how good it would be for them to pit their energies against something challenging and exciting. She understood the value of bringing them away from their old environment and encouraging them to put themselves to the test.

She grinned happily round at Atholl and the boys. 'Nothing to it, is there?' she remarked.

'Well done, there,' said Atholl, looking genuinely impressed. 'We'll have to try a steeper one next time!'

His eyes danced at her, his gaze lingering appreciatively for a second on her petite figure. She was one feisty girl—he knew that it had taken all her courage to do the descent for the first time, and he admired the way she'd kept her fear under control. Someone like her would command the respect of the young lads watching her and he smiled at his own reaction. Why on earth had he imagined that a man would be so much better to be involved on this outward bound course?

Pete had begun his descent, having secured the rope at the top. He was efficient and able, swinging down quickly, but just as he was reaching the ground there was an odd rumbling noise above them. Instinctively they all looked up and watched incredulously as a mini-avalanche of small boulders broke away from an overhang above Pete and started to rain down around him.

Before anyone could move, Zac had raced forward and pushed Pete away from the worst of the fall. Both men fell heavily to the ground, then instinctively coiled their bodies and rolled away from the danger.

Everyone froze for a second then, as if a button had been pressed, they all raced together towards Pete and Zac. Pete was already getting to his feet. His helmet had saved him from the worst of the avalanche, but Zac still lay on the ground. He turned over slowly, his face screwed up in agony.

'Aagh…bloody shoulder,' he groaned. 'I've done something to it. It's agony…'

It seemed to Terry, racing towards the stricken man, that she and Atholl seemed to attract more than their fair share of accidents!

CHAPTER SEVEN

'I DON'T believe this,' muttered Atholl, exchanging a quick look of concern with Terry.

'Let's getting him sitting up,' said Terry. 'We can't see what he's done otherwise.'

Atholl crouched down behind Zac and pointed to Len, the biggest lad there. 'Len, you take the good side and I'll support his back and try to keep his shoulder still while we lift him together. Gently now...'

It was obvious that Zac was in acute pain, and when they'd managed to sit him up, he looked white and shaky, shock kicking in.

'What's happened? Have I broken my arm? You won't touch it, will you?'

'Don't worry, Zac, we just need to look at it carefully. We're not going to do anything to it,' reassured Atholl.

Both doctors looked critically at the injured area, and Terry said after a few seconds of deliberation, 'From the way he's holding his shoulder, I would say he's displaced the head of the humerus—what do you think?'

'What the hell does that mean?' growled Zac, grimacing as he held his arm to his side.

'I'm afraid it means you've probably dislocated your shoulder,' explained Terry. 'Let me cut this T-shirt off so that we can get a proper look. Sorry, it's going to be a bit uncomfortable.'

'It looks like a typical forward dislocation injury,' said Atholl. 'You see, the top of the upper arm bone is like a ball, and it's been forced out of its socket just beneath the acronium. Poor lad.'

'And all because he was helping me,' said Pete, also crouching by Zac. 'You were a star there, Zac. I'm so sorry you're the one that's copped it and not me.' He looked at the two doctors. 'Can we do anything about it?'

'The thing is,' said Terry, 'we really need an X-ray to make sure there isn't an accompanying fracture. Then the treatment is to manoeuvre the head of the humerus back into the socket. I don't think we should attempt to do that without knowing if there's further injury, do you, Atholl?'

He nodded. 'We'd be better to put a sling on and possibly strapping the upper arm to the chest so that it's kept immobilised to minimise pain when he moves.'

Terry looked at the young man assessingly. 'There's no way he can walk back—he's in shock,' she said decisively. 'The sooner we get Zac to hospital, the better.'

'Then we'd better get the mountain rescue people out here. They've got a four-by-four that can get over this moorland without much difficulty…I'll call them now.'

Pete pulled out his mobile phone and stabbed out some numbers. The others all looked rather mournfully at each other—in the twinkling of an eye the day had changed to disaster. Under Terry's supervision they all started putting one or two rucksacks in a supporting wedge round Zac so that he could relax back slightly, although any pressure on the injured side made him wince.

Then Atholl undid his medical pack, taking out the sling he would use to hold Zac's upper arm steady and a big sheet of metallic insulating material to cover the boy and keep him warm. Despite the heat, Zac was shivering with shock.

'Good job we've got the medics with us,' said Len cheerily. 'Otherwise you'd be in a right pickle, mate.'

Zac managed a weak grin. 'I thought coming down the rock would be the most dangerous bit—I didn't realise it was worse on the ground!'

Terry walked back to where her rucksack was and something glinting on the ground by Zac's jacket and spilling half out of a pocket caught her eye. She stopped and looked at it curiously, then bent down and picked it up—it was a pretty Victorian necklace and two little pearl earrings.

Her heart sank and she looked over at Atholl, who had just finished attending to Zac. She walked over to him and said in a low voice, 'Can you just come over here for a moment?'

He looked up, surprised at the urgency in her tone. 'OK. What's the matter?'

She opened her hand and he looked down at the bits of jewellery she was holding.

'Hell,' he muttered slowly. 'These belong to the Mackie sisters, don't they? Where did you find them?'

'Near Zac's jacket by his rucksack,' she replied. 'What do we do now?'

Atholl looked furious, his blue eyes as cold as chips of ice. 'I did hope that these boys would grab this chance to keep on the straight and narrow. What the hell does the boy think he's doing? First smoking dope and now stealing from two old ladies.'

'We're not absolutely sure it's Zac,' pointed out Terry,

putting a calming hand on his arm. 'And if he did, he's not all bad. Look at the way he leapt to save Pete.'

'I know, I know,' said Atholl. 'I'm just exasperated that he can be so damned foolish when he's got the potential to do better things in his life. I'll speak to Pete.'

'Meantime, I'll get the boys to make some tea and they can have something to eat by the river while we wait for this rescue vehicle,' suggested Terry. 'I'll join you in a moment.'

When Pete was shown the evidence of the theft he swore angrily. 'I guess it happened when the boys were doing the sisters' next-door neighbour's garden. There was plenty of time for one of the boys to get into their house.' He looked across at Zac lying uncomfortably against the makeshift support. 'Damn it, I don't want to give up on the lad—he's not all bad. He admitted taking cannabis and he saved me from serious injury. Why the hell did he filch this jewellery?'

'More drugs?' suggested Atholl.

Pete shook his head. 'I don't know about that. Who's he going to sell that necklace to out here? Look, while the others are having lunch we'll just tackle him about this.'

It was almost too easy. Confronted by the evidence of the necklace and earrings, Zac looked almost comically dismayed.

'Why in kingdom come did you take the stuff?' demanded Pete angrily. 'Were you going to buy more drugs?'

'No,' muttered Zac. 'It wasn't like that.'

'What was it like, then?' asked Atholl, frowning at him.

The boy looked mulishly at the ground and was silent. Atholl crouched down opposite him.

'You've let us down, Zac,' he rasped. 'We give you this chance to do something for yourself, use your body and mind in a lovely place, and you throw it back in our faces. Just why the hell did you have to steal from two harmless old ladies, let alone leave a hell of a mess in the room?'

To their amazement a tear rolled slowly down the boy's cheek and he brushed it away impatiently with his good arm. 'I fell over the chair as I was leaving—I didn't have time to clear it up. The jewellery was for my mam. I...I thought it would cheer her up. She never goes out or nothin' like that, and she's not been well. She's stuck inside in that wheelchair all the time. I wanted to take her something back she'd like—she's got nothing pretty.'

'For God's sake, lad, can't you see that, whatever the reason, you're not to steal from anyone?'

Zac looked at the three adults staring at him and said aggressively, 'You don't know what it's like living in that street...there's nothing for anyone there.'

'Yes, we do know, Zac,' said Atholl sharply. 'We came from where you live. We know about the poverty, the broken families—and the parents who do their best in awful circumstances to keep things going. I guess your mother is one of those. She wouldn't want you to mess this up. She knew it was a chance for you to get away from your life in the Gorbals for a little while—prove yourself in a challenge.'

Zac shook his head and muttered, 'I didn't mean to hurt no one...'

There was something pitiful about the boy and Terry felt the fact he wanted to give his mother something she could never have had showed a loving side to his character—if what he said was true.

'Look, Zac, I said after the cannabis incident that you'd go home if you mucked up again,' said Pete grimly.

Zac continued to look sullenly down at the ground. 'So have I got to go?'

Pete sighed. 'You've just saved me from being injured with no thought of your own safety—I think that speaks a lot about you.' He looked at Atholl and Terry. 'If they can manipulate his arm back into place, shall we give him another chance? There's only a short time to go anyway.'

Zac remained gazing down rather like a condemned prisoner. When Atholl and Terry nodded their heads and said in unison, 'One more chance, then,' he looked up, quite startled, as if he hadn't believed he'd ever be given another opportunity.

'It's up to you, Zac,' said Atholl quietly. 'You either go back in disgrace to your mother or stay on the straight and narrow. We've already reported it to the police so I'm afraid you'll have to wait and see if they prosecute you. Perhaps when they hear that you've returned the jewellery and apologised to the Mackies they'll let it pass this time.'

The boy nodded miserably. 'I have let you down, haven't I?' he muttered. 'I like it here—I don't want to mess this up.'

'Well, see you don't, then.' Then Pete's face softened and he patted Zac's good shoulder. 'I'm still very grateful to you for your quick actions, Zac. I know you're a good lad at heart.' He turned round to Atholl and Terry. 'What about some hot, sweet tea for him?'

Terry looked at her watch and said dubiously, 'He may have to be anaesthetised to put his shoulder back—I wouldn't like to jeopardise the timing of that, so perhaps not.'

Pete's mobile started ringing and he pulled it out of his pocket. They saw the expression on his face change to a mixture of amazement and concern as he answered it, then he turned to Atholl and Terry.

'I—I don't believe this,' he stuttered. 'Sal's gone into labour—she's in the hospital now!'

Atholl laughed. 'That's great news, and every cloud has a silver lining, Pete! It's a good job you've got the mountain rescue team coming for Zac—they can take you back with them to the hospital! Terry and I and the lads will go back to The Culleens on foot.'

Pete looked worriedly up the glen where the mountain rescue team would appear from. 'God, I hope they hurry— she could have had it by the time we get there!'

'Calm down, Pete.' Terry smiled. 'It's her first baby—it's going to take a few hours yet!'

'My Sal's never late for anything,' said Pete gloomily. 'I bet it comes quickly!'

It was late at night and the boys had built a campfire when they'd got back to The Culleens down by the loch. The smell of cooking sausages and steak drifted over to Atholl and Terry sitting on the steps of the building away from the others. Len was softly strumming a guitar and Atholl slung his arm carelessly around Terry's shoulders.

'Will you look at those stars? It's a brilliant night,' he murmured. 'It's been a good day, despite poor old Zac's accident—even if we did find out what a fool he's been.'

Two months ago she had been at her lowest ebb, reflected Terry, and now here she was, close up and dangerously near to one of the dishiest and kindest men she'd ever met, in the most romantic setting! She could tell that Atholl was just being casually affectionate. He didn't pull her against him, although every nerve in her body was telling her to put her head on his shoulder. How could she ever have believed that she was in love with Max, concerned only with himself and what he could get out of people? Of course he'd been a conman and duped every-one—including her father.

She looked up at Atholl's firm profile, outlined in the dark, a quiff of dark hair falling over his eyes. What a contrast! Atholl was genuine, she could trust him, she was sure of that. Perhaps that was why she felt so guilty about not being entirely honest with him and what had really brought her up to Scuola. But she couldn't tell him—not just yet, not until she was sure that there would be no repercussions because she'd given her word that she wouldn't divulge a thing.

'You know, I don't think Zac's a bad lad at heart,' she remarked. 'No one who puts his own skin at risk to save someone else's life can be all bad. And perhaps it's almost a reflex action to steal something he thinks will be nice for his mother...'

Atholl looked down at her and smiled. 'I don't think you can imagine the world that Zac and I come from. Sometimes stealing is a way of life when you've nothing—can you under-stand that?'

Stealing a way of life? Terry pulled away from him suddenly, her expression hidden in the shadow of the wall. She understood only too well what he meant.

'Dishonesty isn't confined to the under-privileged,' she said in a strange little voice. 'Surely you know that, Atholl? Just read the newspapers if you want to know about everyone from politicians to solicitors who've strayed from the straight and narrow.'

She stood up and stretched, suddenly wanting to change the subject, to forget about crime and the reasons why people committed it. Atholl looked at her in surprise, sensing the change in her attitude, the raw nerve he seemed to have touched, and that fleeting sadness she sometimes showed.

He was sure it was something to do with this Max who'd let her down—badly hurt her.

Then the sound of a vehicle drawing up by The Culleens made them both turn round and they could see Zac getting out of a taxi.

Terry welcomed the distraction—she didn't want to get drawn into a conversation about criminals.

'Zac! How's the shoulder?' she asked, walking towards him.

Zac grimaced. 'Not so bad, I guess. They've put it in a sling and given me a note to go to my local hospital.'

Atholl joined them and Zac looked at the two doctors rather miserably.

'I...I've something to say,' he muttered. 'I...I'm sorry about the necklace. I'll go and see the old biddies tomorrow. I didn't think about them when I did it. I just thought saw those things on a table when I looked through the window and thought they were pretty wee trinkets.'

'Perhaps you will think now, Zac, before you do something so damn stupid again,' growled Atholl. 'You gave those old sisters a terrible shock. However I know they'll feel better when you've apologised to them—and taken back the jewellery.'

'Will the police bring charges?' The boy's young face looked stricken. 'It'll do me mam's head in if she knows I've been in trouble again. I'll be for the high jump.'

'I don't know. Perhaps if the Mackies speak up for you, you may just get a caution.' Atholl's voice was rough. 'You'll just have to pick yourself up again, Zac. I got into trouble but I managed to turn my life around. You can do the same.'

'I think you've realised what a silly thing it was to do, haven't you, Zac?' said Terry. She was sure the boy was genuinely contrite about what he'd done. 'Now, go and have some of that food the others are barbecuing—you must be very hungry.'

Zac nodded and slouched off, and Atholl sighed as they watched him. 'Who knows? It may possibly have taught him something about being responsible for his own actions. If he'd done this in Glasgow he might never have been caught—perhaps told his mother he'd just found the jewellery or something.'

'I think you're right. He's been caught twice here and he feels a fool.'

There was the sound of another vehicle drawing up, a slamming door and a hearty shout. Everyone turned round and a figure that turned out to be Pete came running towards them in the dark, waving his arms and yelling excitedly.

'Hi, everyone. It's a wee girl! Sally's just given me a beautiful daughter! And they're both absolutely fine!'

After the celebrations, toasting the new baby in beer and wine that Pete had brought back with him, Atholl, Terry and Pete strolled back from the barbecue to the barn. The boys had all turned in and the fire had been damped down. The air was warm, not a breeze stirring the trees by the loch.

'What a day! I'm absolutely shattered. Becoming a father is extremely tiring,' yawned Pete. 'I'm off for some shut-eye. There's spare sleeping bags in the cupboard, so make yourselves at home. You can have my office to sleep in, Terry—there's a camp bed in there, and Atholl can kip with me.'

'Thanks. I'll be along soon,' said Atholl.

Pete disappeared to his room and Terry lingered for a minute, smelling the balmy air of the warm night and listening to the rustlings and little sounds that were part of the surroundings. It seemed so peaceful after the excitement of the day, a time to reflect and wind down. Rather woozily she reflected that perhaps they'd all been a bit too enthusiastic in their celebration of the new baby's birth. The result of drinking a glass or two on a relatively empty stomach had made her feel delightfully relaxed.

She was vaguely aware that Atholl had come to stand by her, looking at her profile as she dreamily watched the night sky.

'What a lovely ending to the day—a new baby arriving!' she murmured.

'Yes—a lovely ending.' His voice was very quiet.

In the silvery light her hair looked fairer, her dark eyes larger. God, she was beautiful. Atholl felt his throat catch at the sweetness of her face, the tip-tilted nose, soft lips and high cheekbones that gave a heart-shaped definition to her face. Since the morning when he'd gone to wake her up in her bedroom, he had become more and more aware as the day had gone on that Terry was everything he wanted—the kind of woman he'd dreamt about but had thought he'd never have a hope in hell of meeting.

When Zara and he had split up, yes, he'd been bruised and mortified—but mostly he'd been furious that she had duped him. If this was what happened when you thought you'd met the right person, he'd vowed he'd be very, very wary before getting involved again. And now Terry had come into his life and the picture was changing rather rapidly.

Atholl bent down, picked a stone up from the shore and skimmed it across the loch, so that it bounced three times and the circles of water rippled out, gleaming in the moonshine. He wondered how long he could go on working and living so close to Terry in a kind of teasing no-man's land where they flirted with each other, then backed off in a tantalising dance. He had to tell her honestly what he felt—and he wanted to know how she felt about him.

'I think I'll turn in now,' Terry said, starting to walk back across the shingly shore.

Atholl put out his hand and took hers, pulling her back slightly. 'Terry…wait a moment. Don't go yet.'

She turned round to him, slightly startled, and then the moon went behind a cloud and for a second they were plunged into almost total darkness. Terry's foot slipped on a smooth rock as she stepped back and she stumbled, almost falling to the ground before Atholl grabbed her, slipping his arm round her waist.

'Careful, we don't want any more accidents today,' he murmured.

Terry giggled, the effect of the wine beginning to kick in rather forcefully.

'You're making a habit of this, catching me when I fall.'

'That's fine by me. I want to be there for you whenever I'm needed.'

'That sounds rather serious,' she said flippantly.

She leant against him for a second, thinking how heavenly it was to relax against the hard wall of his chest, feel the thud of his heart against hers.

'You're very strong,' she teased, the inhibitions she'd had about getting too intimate with Atholl floating away rapidly.

He grinned, his teeth white in the dark. 'I need to be strong, with you falling about all over the place…'

His arms tightened about her and he bent his head to hers, and she felt the evening stubble of his chin prickly against her skin. His lips touched hers gently and it felt like a thousand butterflies were fluttering inside her—then that puritanical voice at the back of her mind whispered that she should march away quickly at this point. With a great effort she pulled away from him, putting a few paces between them.

'We shouldn't do this, Atholl,' she said, rather fuzzily, try- ing to enunciate carefully. 'Let's keep things strictly platonic, then neither of us will get hurt, like I was with Max and you with Zara.'

A moment's silence and then he said harshly, striding forward and catching her arm, 'That's laughable, Terry. You're nothing like that woman. You and she… Why, there's no comparison. She cheated on me, told me so many lies.'

'But everyone has baggage from the past that they might not want to reveal. Atholl, there are things about my background—' she started to say.

Atholl put his finger on her mouth. 'Hush. You're perfect as you are.' His arms tightened around her and he gazed down at her silently for a moment, then murmured, 'There! I've said it! God, Terry, I know you feel something for me too. When we're in the same room it's like there's no one else there—just the two of us. Sparks fly when we're together, honey, admit it!'

He started to kiss her face, covering her brows, her mouth and neck with soft kisses, making her dizzy with delight. She put her arms round his neck and looked into his eyes.

'Yes,' she whispered. 'I admit it.' Had they reached a watershed of some kind on this soft, balmy night? She stroked his thick dark hair back from his forehead and smiled. 'I want to forget about Max and…everything,' she said simply. 'I want to enjoy myself.'

He grinned. 'I'll try and ensure that you will, darling.'

And Terry didn't draw back when he pulled her gently onto the soft mossy ground under the trees by the loch, where the smell was earthy and sweet. He ran his finger down her jaw and her neck, smiling as she responded with a delighted wriggle of her body.

Then he started kissing her face, her lips, trailing his warm mouth down her neck, murmuring her name. Terry felt as if she was back in her dream—Atholl holding her against his chest, his hands stroking her body gently but insistently until every erogenous zone in her body screamed for more.

She lay back on the soft earth and stretched languorously, loving the feel of Atholl's hard muscled body, and the certain knowledge that he was as aroused as she was! Then he knelt up for a second, his legs on either side of her, looking down at her with twinkling eyes.

'What a way to end the evening!'

And Terry laughed because it was exciting and wonderful to undress him as he did her, forget any qualms and enjoy the moment. Funny how quickly it had come to this, she thought dizzily, both of them naked against each other, warm skin against warm skin, his hands doing wonderful things to her body—just as she had dreamt.

Atholl's lips nibbled her ear, and he said throatily, 'You know something—I'm glad I didn't get a man to join the practice.'

She smiled. 'So am I, Atholl, so am I.'

Then they lost themselves in each other, both seizing their moment of happiness, limbs entwined, revelling in the waves of sweetness that swept through them. And afterwards they lay for a long time side by side, under the velvety sky, looking at each other as if almost surprised by the wonder of what they'd just done.

At last Atholl rolled over on his stomach and looked down into Terry's eyes. 'We've been and gone and done it now!' he sighed. 'And just how wonderful it was, my sweet princess!'

Terry looked up at him, seeing his eyes dark and intense in the moonlight, his warm breath on her cheek, and felt a flood of happiness engulf her. It was time to look forward, and she didn't care that she still hadn't told him her full story. She wouldn't worry about that now!

He took her arm as they strolled back together to The Culleens in companionable silence, then he kissed her gently on the steps before she went in.

Atholl stayed outside for a minute, leaning against the wall, gazing across the dark loch with a silver path across it where the moon's light fell. For the first time for many months he felt genuinely at peace with himself and filled with the contentment that came after making love to the most wonderful woman in the world.

He chuckled to himself. He realised that he was in love with Terry, and perhaps he had been since the moment he'd offered her a job the first day she'd come!

CHAPTER EIGHT

TERRY hummed happily as she poured herself a mug of coffee and peered at the computer to see what her list was like for the morning.

Isobel was just finishing a phone call and she turned round to Terry with the slight smile that was the most levity she usually allowed herself.

'Someone's happy,' she remarked. 'So did you have a good weekend, then?'

Only the most wonderful, fantastic day she'd had in her life, thought Terry, a vivid picture of Atholl and her by the loch in the moonlight and the realisation that they both liked each other a lot. Maybe it wouldn't lead to a lifetime's commitment—after all, they'd both had fractured relationships—but suddenly the future looked very bright indeed. She was surprised how calm her voice sounded when she replied.

'Mostly good, thank you, Isobel. On the downside, one of the boys dislocated his shoulder, but Pete's wife gave birth to a little girl at the hospital, which was very exciting. Atholl and I took over for a while when he went to visit Sally.'

Isobel started to pin a notice on the board and didn't speak for a moment. Then she said casually, 'I'm glad you and Atholl get on well—it makes it easier when you work together.'

Was there the slightest emphasis on the words 'work together'? Terry wondered if there was a hidden agenda to Isobel's remarks.

'Yes,' she replied lightly, 'I think we're on the same wavelength when it comes to work.'

Isobel nodded. 'Aye, it's good to see him concentrate on the practice. As you probably know, he had a distressing time with Dr Grahame. It wasn't a good thing for him to mix work with socialising—if you know what I mean. It can lead to all sorts of...shall we say complications? He was most unhappy.'

Was this the gypsy's warning? A caution for her not to get too close to Isobel's darling Atholl? Isobel might be right—work and social pleasure didn't always work out, but if one was careful, surely it needn't be disaster?

'He did tell me about her,' she admitted. 'It was obviously horrible for him.'

Isobel gave a grunt of disgust and started to type something furiously on the computer.

'You could say that. Aye, there were a lot of things Atholl didn't know about that one, and when he did, it was almost too late. Thank God he found out the truth about her.'

Terry bit her lip. What on earth would Isobel say if she really knew what had happened the night before? But a little wave of happiness rippled through her. She really didn't care what Isobel thought!

Sue and Bunty came in, taking off their jackets, and Sue sank into a chair looking her usual harassed self after a weekend looking after her family.

'What a morning! Just try getting three quarrelling boys

off to school on time with all their homework and lunch boxes—and then, just as I think I've got them through the gates, Jake says he's forgotten his sports kit!'

'Have some coffee.' Terry grinned, handing her a cup. 'You can relax now you've come in to work!'

Sue gave a mirthless laugh. 'Relax, did you say? Baby clinic first and then all the check-ups later this morning for the over-fifties. Then this afternoon—'

She was interrupted by a small commotion in the waiting room, a child wailing and an adult's soothing voice saying, 'You'll be all right now.'

'I want my mum. I want her to make it better!' screamed the child over the top of the adult's voice. 'Go and get her *now!*'

'What on earth's happening?' said Isobel sternly, getting up from her chair and marching through to the waiting room. A few seconds later she appeared again, holding a small sobbing boy by the hand.

'Look what I've got, Sue. I think he belongs to you!'

'Jake!' cried Sue in astonishment. She put down her coffee and ran towards the child, cuddling him. 'What's the matter? I've only just dropped you off at school!'

A rather flustered-looking woman appeared at the door. 'I'm afraid Jake's trapped his finger in a door and his nail's gone very black—it looks most painful. I thought it best to bring him straight here, knowing you worked at the medical centre.'

'Mrs Milnthorpe!' Sue turned to the others. 'This is Jake's headmistress. Oh, thank you so much for bringing him here.' She knelt down by her sobbing little boy, who was guarding one hand within the other one. She tried to prise it open. 'Let's have a look, Jake. It's alright, darling, we'll do something about it.' Sue looked up at Terry. 'What do you think? The nail's gone black and it's very swollen.'

Terry looked at the small finger with a purple nail on it proffered very reluctantly for their gaze by the tearful child, and grimaced.

'Poor old Jake! It's obviously bleeding behind the nail and there isn't much space to bleed into, so no wonder it's painful. But don't worry—I've got a great way to make it feel a lot, lot better!'

Jake began to scream. 'I don't want you to touch it. Keep away!' He pulled his hand away from Terry and protected it with his other hand again, looking at them defiantly with tear-filled eyes, then buried his head in his mother's shoulder, squirming when she tried to extricate his arm. Sue looked back at the other women rather helplessly.

'It's not easy when you're related to the patient,' she said wryly.

'Normally the patient isn't using you as a shield!' remarked Terry, squatting down by the little boy and attempting to pull him round to face her. 'Just let me see your poorly finger for a minute, sweetheart. I promise it won't hurt,' she said.

A muffled bellow was all she got in reply.

'Well, well, now—is somebody in trouble here?' said a familiar deep voice.

Atholl's tall figure was looming at the door. He looked around at everyone clustered round the little boy, his eyes holding Terry's for a second of intimate scrutiny so that her pulse bounded into overdrive. Then, quickly assessing the situation, he strode over to the little boy and bent down beside him. He prised the child away from his mother gently but firmly, taking no notice of the child's resistance or the increasing volume of his screams.

'Come on, wee lad,' he said coaxingly, a mixture of understanding and rallying in his voice. 'You're a brave boy, I know.'

He held the frightened child close to him, patting his back, letting the little boy calm down as naturally as if it had been his own son, thought Terry. She sighed, remembering how tender her father had been to her when she had been little, always on her side, always there for her when she'd needed him.

Atholl was still speaking to the little boy. 'Let Dr Terry and I get rid of that pain for you.' He looked up at Terry with a wink. 'We make a magical team, you know!'

Terry leapt back into the present, pushing the flashback away. Atholl delved into his jacket pocket and brought out a tiny model car, waving it in front of Jake.

'See this, Jake. Look, when I push it along the floor the headlamps light up—can you see them?'

There was a moment's silence as the little boy's interest was caught, following the toy with his eyes as it raced along until stopped by a chair leg.

'Would you like that, Jake?' The child nodded silently. 'Well, just let Dr Terry look at that finger for a minute, then it's all yours.'

'Right—has anyone got a match?' asked Terry. 'I've got the rest of the equipment in my bag. Here it is…a pin and a pair of tweezers!'

Isobel came forward with a box of matches and everyone watched goggled-eyed as Terry gripped the pin in the tweezers and then held the tip in the flame of the match. Atholl had a firm arm round Jake and he swivelled the child round so that he was pointing towards the window, and at the same time held the little boy's hand out towards Terry.

'Look, Jake,' he said urgently. 'Can you see that squirrel running up the tree outside? He's just stolen some nuts from the bird table out there...'

During the time that Jake's attention was diverted, Terry took his finger and pressed the glowing pin tip firmly into the injured nail. There was a faint hiss as the hot metal burnt a hole in the nail and blood started to ooze out through the freshly made aperture.

'Oh,' breathed Bunty, impressed. 'That was neatly done! How amazing!'

Terry laughed. 'Not to be done at home, but it worked because Mrs Milnthorpe got Jake here before the blood began to clot.'

Jake twisted round and looked at his finger doubtfully, then back at the adults round him. 'It's not hurting now!' he said wonderingly.

'I told you that Dr Terry and I are good when we get together!' Atholl's mischievous eyes met Terry's, and she looked away hastily. Did he want the whole room to know about them?

'I think brave boys deserve a chocolate biscuit and some milk,' she said quickly. 'And then you can go back to school—that finger won't give you any trouble now!'

'I'll take you back,' said Mrs Milnthorpe. 'You will have a lot to tell your friends, won't you? Quite a hero!'

After a farewell hug from his mother, Jake trotted off quite happily, clutching the little car, and Sue sank back into a chair, blowing out her cheeks.

'That child—he's always getting into scrapes,' she sighed. 'Thank you so much, both of you, for that procedure! By the way, Atholl, do you carry a stock of those little cars?'

'It's like a toy shop in my pockets.' He grinned. 'Anything else we can do for you?'

Sue's eyes twinkled. 'Well, I hate to mention it…but as a matter of fact I thought one of you was going to clear some rubbish from your room this weekend so that I could transfer some of *my* rubbish in the space you'd made! There's still only just enough space in my room for one thin patient and me at the moment!'

Terry clapped her hand to her forehead. 'Oh, God—so sorry, Sue! Er…I'm afraid it just went out of my head completely. You know we had The Culleens outward bound course yesterday and then Pete's baby arrived…and one thing and another…'

'I know, I know.' Sue smiled good-naturedly. 'I'm sure your mind was on plenty of things other than The Sycamores!'

How right she was, thought Terry wryly, almost able to feel the mischievous grin that played across Atholl's face! She averted her gaze quickly—all these double entendres were getting embarrassing!

'I promise I'll do it this evening—honest,' she said.

'Would you like me to help you sort things out?' asked Sue.

'No, I'll be fine. I've got to be really ruthless—there seem to be loads of ancient files stacked in a corner which I'm sure are completely out of date. Atholl's uncle obviously doesn't like throwing things out!' She turned to go to her room. 'Right, I'll get on with some of the BP checks now—would you bring the blood test results and post when you've got them, Bunty?'

Janet Rathbone was her first patient that day, small, slight and softly spoken, in complete contrast to her husband, thought Terry with amusement. He had obviously managed to persuade her to come in for a blood-pressure check. She had a large bruise on her cheek below her eye, and resembled a little bird, looking at Terry with her head cocked on one side.

'That bruise looks painful,' Terry observed, as she prepared to take the woman's blood pressure.

'I walked into the glass door of the hotel dining room,' explained Mrs Rathbone. 'Very clumsy of me—I was deep in thought.' She smiled pleasantly at Terry. 'I hope you're enjoying life here, Dr Younger. I believe you've taken over from Dr Brodie's uncle?'

'That's right. And, yes, I love it here on Scuola. Now, if I could just ask you a few questions about your general health to update our records?'

'If you wish—but I'm very lucky,' replied Janet. 'Some people, like my poor husband, seem to have to visit the doctor a lot. I've been blessed with a very strong constitution.'

Was there a twinkle in her eyes as she said this? wondered Terry. She knew her husband better than anyone and was well aware of his worries over his health. Janet herself did indeed look healthy—no tremors, a good colour, strong nails and, listening to her heart through her stethoscope, a good, regular beat.

'That's great. I suppose you keep up with dental checks, eye examinations, and so?'

The slightest hesitation made Terry look up at the woman questioningly.

'I will make sure I do,' Mrs Rathbone assured her quickly. 'I have been meaning to have my eyes checked.'

A glimmer of an idea occurred to Terry and she opened a drawer and pulled out an eye chart. She hooked it up on the wall behind the desk.

'Can you read me those lines as far down as you can go?' she asked.

There was a silence, and then very slowly the woman began to read the first line, petering out after a few letters. 'I…I'm sorry. It does seem a little blurred.'

'Do you wear glasses for distance, Mrs Rathbone?'

'No, no, my sight's always been fine.'

'What about reading glasses?'

'Oh, I've never needed them…'

Terry reached into a drawer and pulled out the *Scuola Recorder* that Bunty had given her a few days ago, showing Mrs Rathbone the large photo on the front page.

'By the way, have you seen this?' she asked. 'See anyone you know?'

The woman peered at it, screwing her eyes up, then said at last. 'It's not a very clear photograph… Is it Dr Atholl? It's a bit like him…'

Terry leant back in her chair and smiled across at Mrs Rathbone, pretty sure that she knew what was causing Mrs Rathbone's clumsiness.

'I'm sure there's nothing to worry about, but I have to say I think you really do need glasses. Your sight has probably deteriorated since you last had an eye test—quite normal for everyone to get changes in their sight as they get older.'

'To be honest, I've never actually *had* an eye test, although I did begin to wonder why things didn't seem to be as clear as they were. In fact,' Janet admitted, 'I really don't do any reading now—no time, I suppose. Frankly, I don't really hold with all this worrying about health and testing all the time.'

'Well, while you're here, let me just have a quick look at your eyes,' said Terry, taking her ophthalmoscope out of a drawer. 'I'm by no means an expert on eyes, of course, but I can get a general idea of their health.'

Through the instrument Terry could see the entire area of
the retina, the head of the optic nerve and the retinal arteries,
all being illuminated by a perforated angled mirror.

'It all seems to be fine,' she said reassuringly, putting the
instrument down. 'But please do make an appointment to see
an optician pretty soon. Don't think that somehow you're
"giving in" by having glasses. To be honest, on the basis of
reading that chart, you shouldn't drive without them.'

Janet looked with slight embarrassment at Terry. 'Oh
dear—how very remiss of me... I should have realised that—
both my parents had very poor sight.' Then with a burst of
candour she said, 'The thing is, Doctor, Cyril is a great one
for his health and the more he goes on about what he might
have wrong with him, the more I seem to want to prove that
I'm in the peak of condition!'

Terry laughed. 'And I'm sure you are! You're very
slim—no weight worries. I'll take your BP now, but I bet
it's normal.'

'I promise to make an eye appointment. I have put things
like that off because this is our busiest time of year at the hotel,
of course, but I realise how important it is to have my eyes
checked,' said Janet when Terry had finished.

She picked up her handbag and got up from the chair. 'One
thing, though, Doctor. Please don't say anything to Cyril—
he'll only say he told me so and never let me forget it! I shall
pretend I'm going to the optician off my own bat!'

'Whatever goes on between us is strictly confidential,' assured
Terry. 'But please come to see us if you don't feel well, even if
you do feel you've got to prove something to your husband!'

So that was that, thought Terry wryly as the woman went
out. In fact, it was a very good thing that Cyril had persuaded

his wife to come in for a check-up before she had a major accident—there were definitely times when it paid to be fussy!

It was a busy morning and Terry made one or two house calls during her lunch-hour before dashing back to a mother and baby clinic at two o'clock. By three-thirty she was back in her room, stretching her stiff back and yawning as Bunty came in with a pile of papers in one hand and a cup of tea in the other.

'Here's the blood tests,' she said cheerily. 'And lots of mail to keep you occupied. And a cup of tea to wake you up—I saw that yawn!'

Terry laughed. 'I could just flake out now,' she admitted. 'That tea's really welcome. I'll make a start on the paperwork now.'

Then Terry's intercom buzzed and Bunty put the papers down on the desk and went out.

'When you're free, can I have a word?' asked Atholl.

'Yes. I'm just going to get to grips with some paperwork.'

She looked up as Atholl came into the room, a familiar rush of desire and happiness mingling when she saw him. He stood for a second looking at her from the doorway, dark hair standing up in little peaks over his forehead, his blue eyes smiling at her. Then he strode over to her, looking down with a tender smile.

'Was last night wonderful or what, sweetheart?'

Then, before she could answer, he held her face in his hands and kissed her full and passionately on her lips.

'For God's sake, Atholl—we're at work!' she protested, half laughing and putting her hands on his shoulders to push him away.

'I know,' he said imperturbably. 'So what? Just a friendly

greeting! You left pretty promptly this morning. I thought
you might have been tired and had a lie-in after last night…'
He looked mischievously into her eyes.

'I certainly had a good night's sleep,' she said rather primly.

'I wonder why that should be?' he teased.

And Terry smiled up at him radiantly. 'It was wonderful
Atholl, but we must cool it in the office.'

'I'm just being friendly,' he murmured, pulling her up from
her chair, and kissing her neck and cleavage with soft butter-
fly kisses that sent little electric shocks of pleasure through
her body. And, of course, her good resolutions were forgotten, and she responded ardently, allowing him to tease her lips
open, arching her body against his, feeling his hands caressing her curves, until she knew that unless he stopped fairly
soon she might throw caution to the winds and allow him to
make love to her on the floor of her surgery! He drew away
with a chuckle and held her at arm's length for a second, his
eyes dancing with amusement.

'I'd love to finish this off properly, my sweet, but perhaps,
as you said, this room isn't quite the right place during
surgery hours…'

Terry laughed. 'Saved by the bell! I had visions of Isobel
coming in and finding us—and I don't think she's too keen
on you having female followers!'

Atholl grinned. 'She regards me as a surrogate son and
after my experience with Zara she's like a Rottweiler where
my welfare is concerned! However, back to work, I'm afraid.
We've got a potential worry at the Caledonian Hotel.'

Terry frowned. 'Isn't that the place that belongs to the
Rathbones? Janet was my first patient this morning.'

'Poor woman—she'll be very worried at the moment. They

had a small wedding party there at lunchtime and one or two
of the guests collapsed shortly after eating the lunch.'

'Oh, no! Food poisoning, I suppose?'

'It's all rather mysterious—not the usual symptoms, from
what I can gather. The victims have been taken to hospital but
the public health people will be some time getting across
from the mainland, so I'm afraid it's up to you and I to go and
take samples of everything in the kitchen to get them analysed
as quickly as possible. I've telephoned through to say that the
kitchen must be sealed off until we get there.'

Terry grabbed her medical bag, and put the e-mails and post
to one side of the computer—she would look at them later.

'What are the symptoms?' asked Terry as they drove over
to the hotel.

'Pretty grim—numbness, a weak pulse, thirst, and two of
the victims have had convulsions and paralysis of the limbs,'
said Atholl. 'The last thing a place like Scuola needed with
the start of the vital tourist season is an outbreak of illness in
a hotel—the sooner we can trace its cause, the better.'

The Caledonian Hotel looked out over the Scuola Sound and
had pretty gardens surrounding it. As they drove up, Terry could
see a young couple playing tennis on a court at the side of the
hotel and at the front was a beautifully mown lawn with croquet
hoops on it. Everything looked immaculate and cared for.

'It's very popular with holidaymakers and the locals,' explained Atholl as they got out of the car. 'Whatever one can say
about Cyril as a patient, he and Janet work like the devil—it
must be quite stressful. They have an excellent chef and the
food's terrific. I just hope to goodness they haven't got salmo-
nella or the like on their hands—it could ruin their reputation.'

Janet met them at the door, her face showing the strain of the past few hours. 'Thank you for coming so quickly,' she said. 'I'm so worried, we seem to have an outbreak of some kind on our hands. I can't believe it's food poisoning—we're absolutely meticulous about everything that's produced here.'

Atholl patted her shoulder kindly. 'I know how careful you are, Janet. Try not to worry. We'll go straight to the kitchen and start taking samples straight away—it could be something that's been brought in from outside. Nobody's disturbed anything, have they?'

Janet trotted along beside them, her words tumbling over each other. 'It was awful. They simply started shaking and collapsed about half an hour after eating. At first we thought one of them was having a heart attack as he suffers from angina, but it was soon obvious that it was affecting quite a few of them. Oh, what can it be?'

'What had they been eating?' asked Terry.

Janet looked a little tearful. 'The wedding party had roast beef, and Cyril and I had a roast beef sandwich for an early lunch—but we haven't been affected.'

'We'll get the samples for analysis now, and then go over to the lab at the hospital to get them done as soon as possible and look at the victims while we're there.'

It took a good hour to go through everything in the kitchen, collect all the samples and then rush them to the hospital laboratory.

'We'll try and get them done today,' said the technician. 'Everyone's going to work flat out.'

'Then let's sit down and make a definitive list of absolutely everything these people ate this lunchtime—to the smallest thing,' suggested Atholl, pulling a pen from his pocket. 'One good thing—no one seems in immediate danger although it would be very helpful if we knew the cause.'

It seemed to be a fairly random attack—a husband would be affected, but not the wife, a parent, but not a child. They interviewed everyone they were able to at the hospital, and Terry observed in a puzzled way when they were back in the hotel office with the Rathbones, 'Everyone seems to have had the same—roast beef.' She looked at the list they'd made, tracing the ticks against each name. 'There's only one thing I can see that differs from one group to the other, and that's the fact that some had the horseradish sauce and others didn't.'

Atholl stared at her for a moment, then said slowly, 'You know, you may be on to something there. It's a long shot, but at the back of my mind a bell's ringing. I think it's time we interviewed the chef!'

'What do you think it is?' asked Terry curiously.

'I can't be sure—it seems almost too far fetched, but I have come across it once before,' replied Atholl cryptically, striding through to the kitchens with Terry and the Rathbones behind him.

Bernie, the chef, was defensive when questioned. 'Everything I serve is home prepared—the meats from local suppliers, the vegetables are from the kitchen garden—'

'Ah, yes, the vegetables,' interrupted Atholl. 'Where do you get your horseradish sauce from?'

'As I told you,' said Bernie proudly, 'it's all home made. The horseradish grows in the garden.'

'Then let's go into the kitchen garden and see the exact spot you got the roots from,' said Atholl. He paused and asked Cyril and Janet, 'Tell me, when you had your roast beef sandwiches, did you have horseradish sauce with them?'

Cyril and Janet Rathbone looked at each other in puzzlement. 'No, we don't like spicy hot stuff,' said Cyril. 'Don't tell me it's something to do with that?'

Atholl didn't reply but went with Bernie into the walled garden where the vegetables were grown. At the far end there had been some excavation work to demolish a shed and the ground was fairly churned up.

'Show me the roots you used,' said Atholl.

Bernie bent down and pulled up the familiar horseradish roots from the disturbed soil and handed them to Atholl, who scratched their surface and sniffed them, then smiled rather grimly.

'I think we've found the culprit,' he said looking up at them. 'These tubers look like horseradish roots but, in fact, I'd bet my life they're aconite or monksbane, which is highly toxic. It's very easy to confuse the two roots, especially when the earth is churned about and the familiar leaves have been trampled on.'

There were quick indrawn breaths of amazement from the others.

'What made you think of it?' asked Terry.

'When I was working in A and E we had a similar case. It's a few years back now, but when I heard that word "horseradish" it brought it back to me. A farmer's wife supplemented her income by making sauces and chutneys and had made the same mistake.'

'Oh, my God!' said Bernie in a broken voice. He turned ashen and sat down suddenly on a bench. 'I'd no idea... I...I can't believe I nearly killed all those people...'

'It wasn't you who picked the roots,' cut in Janet suddenly. 'It was me. I just handed them to you.' She turned to Terry, her face a white mask of horror. 'Perhaps it was because of my bad vision. I didn't notice the difference in the leaves…'

Atholl shook his head. 'As you saw, the ground had been so churned up, there were no leaves, and the tubers of both plants are very similar.'

The Rathbones and Bernie looked completely shocked. Terry said briskly, 'Look, no one's in danger. I've just rung A and E and I think we can breathe a sigh of relief. If it's confirmed that Atholl's right, they'll know what they're dealing with. I imagine that people only had a tiny bit of the sauce because it would have tasted rather peculiar.'

'I…I'd no idea that we had monksbane,' said Janet miserably. 'I hope it won't ruin our reputation…we've worked so hard to get this place on its feet. I couldn't bear it if the whole thing went down again.'

'I don't think so,' said Atholl gently. 'It's a harsh lesson but now you know all in the garden isn't necessarily roses, I'm sure you'll never make that mistake again. Look,' he added cheerfully, 'I'm not in the least worried—in fact, I'd like to book Dr Younger and I in for a meal tomorrow night!'

Janet looked at him in grateful surprise. 'Of course—and it'll be on the house!'

Atholl shook his head firmly. 'Oh, no, we'll pay our way. What do you say, Terry?'

'Sounds a great idea to me.' Terry grinned. 'And I can't wait to taste your roast beef!'

The next day Terry came into the surgery early to deal with the paperwork she'd been unable to look at the day before because of the incident at the Caledonian Hotel. There was a message from Atholl to say that the laboratory had confirmed that aconite had been found in the horseradish sauce sample and that the patients were all doing well—and that he was looking forward to their dinner together that evening!

Terry sat down in front of the usual pile of circulars from drug companies, medical magazines and letters that came in on a daily basis, sorting them out with a light heart. She mused rather distractedly on what she would wear that evening. Her wardrobe was decidedly meagre, and she decided to nip out during the lunch-hour on the off chance that the small dress shop in Scuola had anything remotely glamorous she could buy.

One of the letters was a private one, with a handwritten envelope. Odd, that—she never received personal mail nowadays. After all, no one knew where she lived, except her father's solicitor, and that would surely be typewritten.

She turned the envelope over in her hand. There was just the barest address there. 'Dr T. Younger, GP on Scuola.' There was something familiar about the handwriting.

Curiously she slit open the envelope and pulled out a note together with a newspaper clipping—it was the article and photograph about her and Atholl rescuing the baby from the quayside the first day she'd arrived in Scuola. It had obviously been taken up by a national newspaper.

She read the note slowly, hardly comprehending it at first, then reread it with mounting horror. Her mouth suddenly went very dry and her heart started to thump uncomfortably, the light-hearted happiness she'd felt a moment ago draining away from her. She put the note down and stared at it, huddled back against her chair.

'My God,' she whispered. 'What on earth can I do?'

She got up and walked unsteadily over to the window,

drawing aside the blind and looking out at the view of the hills and the sea beyond. She was so happy here—happier than she could ever have imagined, coming to a place that was new to her and leaving all she'd known behind. Life was interesting, the people were friendly, and, of course, above all there was Atholl, a man that she knew now that she'd fallen for, hook, line and sinker, in the few weeks she'd been here.

Was all that going to be put in jeopardy because her past had suddenly and horribly caught up with her?

CHAPTER NINE

She let the blind go with a snap and went back to the desk, sitting down with her head in her hands, trying to remain calm, to think about what she ought to do. She took up the piece of paper again and reread it, as if by so doing it would be different this time.

Hi, darling,
Bet you didn't think that I'd be in touch with you! No wonder this photo caught my eye immediately—you can change your name but not your looks, even if your hair is shorter! It's amazing how news travels fast, even when it's from a little place like Scuola, isn't it? Now I know where you live, I've come up to the area to have a little chat with you, but mostly to warn you I need some ready cash—a few thousand would help. I'd like you to get this a.s.a.p. I'll give you four days to organise cash in used notes. Better if you keep your mouth shut about this, sweetheart. If you don't, your nice Dr Brodie might get hurt (accidentally of course).
Be seeing you, Max.

Terry shuddered. That damn newspaper! Even though she thought she'd disguised her looks well, had convinced herself that nobody would guess where she was, and had begun to feel relaxed in her life here, Max had found her! The man she'd once thought she'd loved so much had found out where she was and was blackmailing her.

She put her head in her hands, the whole dismal scenario of what had happened to her father reeling through her mind. She'd thought she was so safe up here in Scuola—but it seemed there was to be no hiding place from the implied threats in that horrible little note. And Atholl was in as much danger as she was—she was under no illusion about what Max was capable of. Her father had paid a high price for her involvement with Max because Max didn't care who he hurt.

What the hell could she do? She leaped up from her chair and started pacing about the room, trying to control her panic.

One thing was certain—she couldn't put Atholl at risk by staying at his cottage any longer. In fact, it would be better altogether if they ended their relationship, she thought miserably. He mustn't in any way be sucked into the vile and corrupt world that Max represented. She could imagine Max demanding money from Atholl, and threatening to harm her if Atholl didn't agree.

She would have to inform the police, although it was hard to see how letting them know about this grubby little note would do any good. There weren't many policemen on the island and they could hardly give her twenty-four-hour protection. She would have to move on.

She took the note and put it in her handbag, snapping it shut viciously. She had been naive to think that she wouldn't be discovered—letting herself be photographed for the paper had been a careless mistake. With cold logic she realised that realistically her only option was to leave Scuola and get as far away from Atholl as she could. She could face Max herself but she was damned if Atholl was going to be mixed up in this sordid scenario.

A lump of sadness lodged somewhere in her throat. How could she leave her lovely life here? But Max was her problem, not Atholl's, and she must make her own decisions. It had been too good to be true anyway, she mused sadly. Happiness such as she had started to experience lately could never last—the past had been bound to catch up with her. Somehow she had to be strong and tell Atholl that it was over between them and that she was leaving Scuola.

Atholl was already home when she returned to the cottage.

'Hi, sweetheart.' He smiled, his whole face lighting up as his eyes wandered over her. 'Let's get going—I'm starving! Go and put on your glad rags. Oh, by the way, we're needed in Hersa tomorrow morning—that's the little island I pointed out to you. There's been a case of meningitis affecting a child who was visiting her grandparents on the mainland, and all the children who may have come into contact with her need to be given antibiotics pronto. It needs two of us again, so I'd be much obliged if you'd come with me. Sue's already involved with doing MMR vaccinations here at the baby clinic.'

He waited expectantly for her reply. What could she say? It was an emergency after all.

'Yes…yes, of course I'll come,' she said distractedly.

She closed her eyes briefly, trying to compose herself, psych herself up to tell him that their affair was over and an intimate and romantic dinner with him was not on that evening.

'Atholl, I, er…' She paused for a second, gathering her courage, then swallowed hard and said in a rapid voice, 'Atholl, I can't go out with you tonight.'

He looked at her in surprise. 'Why not?'

She sat down at the little kitchen table and gripped her hands together. 'Because…because I've something I've got to tell you as soon as possible. It's very hard to say this. It…it's about us…'

Atholl looked at her with twinkling eyes. 'Oh, dear, you sound very serious, sweetheart. What is it about us?'

God, this was difficult! Terry twisted her hands together wretchedly. How could she put it to him that although they'd made wonderful love only the evening before, now she wanted to finish their liaison, leave her job?

'The thing is…' she started haltingly. 'The thing is, I think we've been too hasty, Atholl. I…I've been thinking it over and I don't feel I can get involved in a relationship at the moment. It's too soon after Max…I've been too impetuous.'

Atholl sat down on the chair opposite her, his expression changing slowly from humour to incredulity. 'What the hell are you talking about?'

'I…I mean I've just had one intense relationship. I can't leap into another one so quickly.'

'You mean you think you're on the rebound?' He laughed and said in amusement, 'Are you trying to say it's over between us? Good God, we've only just started.'

'I know, I know! That's why I think it's best to stop things before we get too…committed.'

Those amazing eyes bored into hers and she looked away hastily. 'This seems to have come on very quickly. I didn't notice you holding back yesterday when I kissed you in the surgery,' he commented quietly.

'I had time to think about it when I was clearing things out in my room for Sue. It suddenly came over me,' Terry replied helplessly.

'Come on, sweetheart,' he said gently. He reached across the desk and took her hand. 'We don't have to break up. We can just take things a little more slowly if you feel a bit over-whelmed by it all. As a matter of fact, I also feel as if a steam-roller's gone over me—it's been an incredible experience!' He grinned at her. 'Perhaps you feel that, like fine wine, we should savour what we feel, not gulp it down too greedily!'

Terry drew her hand from his and said dully. 'No...half-measures are no good, Atholl.'

He frowned, then said flatly, 'I don't believe you. What's brought this on?'

'I told you—it's too soon after my involvement with Max. I'm in a muddle about my feelings.'

'For God's sake...' Atholl got up from the chair and paced up and down, looking across at her in bewilderment. 'You said Max was a bastard, only wanting what he could get. I'd have thought he was easy enough to get out of your system.' He stood still for a moment, gazing down at her, his eyes like two blue chips of steel lasering their way into her.

'I...I can't switch on and off like that,' said Terry wretch-edly. 'I need space, Atholl. I want to move from the cottage and lead a completely separate life. In fact...' Her voice trembled slightly. 'I think it's better if I leave the practice. It would be incredibly hard to work so closely with you after what's gone on between us and then to go on as...as mere colleagues.'

He shook his head, then came round the table and put his hand under her chin and tilted her face to his. 'What's gone wrong, darling?' he asked softly. 'Only a couple of days ago you and I were in each other's arms, making wonderful love. We had the most magical night together. I shall never forget it…'

He pulled her towards him and took her face in his hands, kissing her with tender gentleness, then putting his arms around her and holding her so close to him that she could feel his hip bones next to hers, his heart thumping against her breast. God, what she would have given to have told him everything, to have made love to him then and there!

Terry gritted her teeth. She had to be tough, no good being half-hearted about this, although it was like cutting off her right arm. She tried to pull herself away from him, but he held onto her with a grip of steel, looking down at her with his incredible eyes.

'Don't tell me Sunday night meant nothing to you, Terry,' he said huskily.

'Of course not. I enjoyed it very much Atholl.'

Atholl's hands dropped to his sides abruptly, and he stepped back a pace.

'Enjoyed it?' he exploded, staring at her incredulously for a second, then he sank back into the chair, shaking his head. 'I thought it would mean more to you than eating an ice cream.'

'As I said, once I realised I didn't want total commitment, I decided it was better to finish things promptly. You once mentioned that relationships between doctors didn't work, and perhaps you're right—better not to risk it.'

Atholl laughed shortly. 'For God's sake, that was a throwaway remark, a joke, sweetheart.'

'I…I feel I'm not sure about anything at the moment. It wouldn't be fair to lead you on like Zara did and then let you down.' Terry's voice was stony, unemotional. It was the only way she could do it.

'Don't bring Zara Grahame into this,' he said roughly. 'I thought you loved it here, even before we got together. You told me you loved the people, the countryside,' he added. 'And I thought you loved me a little too.'

Terry licked her dry lips, and said nothing. It was too dreadful: she was telling lie after lie. Of course she loved him, more than ever now, and that was why she had to cut herself off from Atholl and any danger she might put him in.

There was a long silence, then Atholl stood up again abruptly, his expression becoming cold and his mouth a grim line. 'I see. I didn't realise it was just to be a one-night stand...'

'No! It wasn't—it wasn't anything like that!' Terry cried. The words dragged out of her. 'I just need time to think... without being too near you.'

'You've made your mind up pretty quickly.' His voice was grating. 'And where do you propose to stay in the meantime before you leave the area? The flat here isn't ready yet.'

'I'll go to a B and B I've seen down the road for the time being.'

'Got it all planned, haven't you?'

She looked down at the table, trying to control the tell-tale tears that threatened to engulf her. 'I think it's best, Atholl. You wouldn't want me to be with you unless I was sure, would you?'

'Of course not,' he said with cold politeness. 'You must do what you think fit. I presume you'll take your things fairly soon, then.'

Atholl walked towards the door, turning round just before he opened it. 'I take it you're still working with me here for a little while to give me time to get someone else?'

'Yes,' she whispered. 'But the sooner the better—for both our sakes.'

There was bafflement and grief in the look he gave her, and Terry had a sudden urge to run towards him and fling herself in his arms and tell him that she loved him more than anything else in the world, but she nodded wordlessly, aware that if she said anything she would burst into tears. She heard him bang out of the house, shutting the front door with a crash and then driving down the road with a roar of acceleration.

She shook her head helplessly. She'd gone about this all the wrong way. She should have left as soon as she'd got the note, disappeared out of Atholl's life completely and just written to him later. But she was too selfish, wasn't she? She needed to try and give him some explanation so that he wouldn't think too badly of her, so that he would have time to get help with the practice. As it was, he probably despised her for leading him on and then abandoning him.

She ran upstairs to the little bedroom where she'd been so happy and started stuffing her clothes into her suitcase, sobbing her heart out.

What the hell had gone wrong? Atholl changed gear savagely as he accelerated up the road and into the hills, trying to make sense of the conversation he'd just had with Terry. His thoughts flickered back to their love-making on the shore of the lake by The Culleens. He could swear that the passion and happiness she'd shown then with him hadn't been made up. He could, perhaps, understand that she might want to take things slower—their attraction to each other had been like a thunderbolt, unable to keep their hands off each other. But to finish completely? To leave the practice? It just didn't add up, he thought.

He parked the car at the top of the hill in the little glade he'd taken Terry to on her first day of work, and got out, trying to clear his head in the fresh air. Perhaps, he mused bitterly, he was just a bad judge of women, and he'd learned nothing from his experience with Zara. But deep down he was sure there was something more to this than Terry wanting to take things more slowly. How could she finish a relationship so abruptly when he just knew that what they felt for each other was so strong? His face hardened as he stared unseeingly down at the blue waters of the Scuola Sound. He wouldn't give up on her yet, not while she still remained on the island. He had to find out what was behind this devastating change of mind.

It was such a beautiful morning as the little ferry made its way to Hersa over the calm Scuola Sound. The sea shimmered in the golden sunlight and a flock of terns skimmed over the water to the side of the boat. Terry leaned miserably against the rail and watched the island come closer, unaware of the beauty all around her, her thoughts completely taken up with the horrible situation she found herself in. It was bad enough that that bastard Max was out there somewhere, hunting her, trying to silence her. Almost worse than that was the fact that she had finished things between her and Atholl and she couldn't explain to him the true reason why she'd done it.

Atholl was standing at the other side of the deck, his back to her, ramrod straight. He had merely nodded briefly to her when she'd arrived on the quayside. Now he was on his mobile phone and had started pacing up and down, and Terry could sense his restless energy and the anger he felt sparking off towards her.

He put the phone back in his pocket and folded his arms,

looking at the wake creaming behind them and smiling grimly to himself. His mother had just informed him she was coming to stay for a few days soon and he could well imagine what she would say if she knew what had happened between him and Terry. 'She's out of your league, son. She doesn't want to be involved with a boy from the Gorbals. I could have told you this would happen!'

Perhaps that was it. His mother would see what he could not, blinded as he was by attraction for Terry. Terry must suddenly have realised that she was hitching herself to someone from a completely different world from his. He gazed stonily over the water, his lips set in a firm line. He wouldn't have thought it of Terry—she had seemed so fresh, so straightforward—but, then, what did he know about women? He'd made one bad mistake so the odds were that he could easily make another.

And yet…he turned round and looked at Terry standing by the rail, her slender figure looking vulnerable, her short fair hair whipping across her elfin face. He'd thought he'd known her so well—she seemed to be the last person in the world who would be concerned with something as trivial as the background one would come from, and he couldn't really believe that she felt that about him.

At that moment she turned round and looked at him, and her expression had such pain and sadness in it that he could swear that she still felt something for him. She had been so intransigent about them parting and yet he couldn't believe that that was what she really wanted.

What was he to do? He couldn't force Terry to change her mind, but he was damned if he'd just sit back and let her go away without a fight. And he'd find out the cause of this sudden change of heart if it was the last thing he did.

Terry went over to a bench and sat down. It was no good regretting what she'd done—it was the only option that she could see. She had contacted the police and they were aware of the situation, giving her a special number to ring if she felt threatened. It hadn't made her feel any safer.

They were drawing up to the little dockside now and the ropes had been thrown over the bollards to hold the ferry steady. Atholl was pushing his motorbike down the ramp and Terry followed him, horribly aware that she would have to get on the back of it and cling to him when they rode to the clinic. The last thing she needed was to be as close to him as that, holding onto his muscled body, awakening all kinds of feelings she was trying to suppress.

'Put this on,' he said unsmilingly as he handed her a crash helmet.

She took it wordlessly and then climbed onto the pillion seat behind him. He stamped on the accelerator and they whirled off. Terry closed her eyes and gritted her teeth as she pressed against him—so close to him physically and yet already so far from him emotionally. She had hurt him desperately, she knew, and he was angry and frustrated at her inexplicable change of heart. His manner had become cold and distant even now as if to cut himself off from her—and who could blame him? He must feel he hadn't had much luck with women, reflected Terry miserably.

They stopped outside a small building with the words 'Hersa Community Hall' across the front, where a queue of children with parents were going in. Atholl and Terry got off the bike and he propped it up against the wall and took out a bag from underneath the pillion seat.

'Come on,' he said brusquely. 'Let's get this done.'

There were plenty of children there, some from one of the other tiny inhabited islands near Hersa but who attended the local school. Their parents were all extremely worried and a lot of reassurance had to be given that their offspring were highly unlikely to contract meningitis and that the antibiotics were merely a precaution.

Sitting so close to Atholl and working steadily through their young patients, it would seem to the outsider that there was nothing amiss between them, reflected Terry. Atholl was courteous to her when he spoke, but had introduced her to the parents as 'Dr Younger, who is just filling in for my uncle for a short time'. When he said that, his eyes caught hers for a second and there was mutual misery in their locked gazes. Terry turned away abruptly to deal with her next small patient, a little boy with a snub nose and freckles.

'And your name is…?' she asked him.

'Jimmy Scott, miss.' He grinned at her as she gave him the injection, seemingly unaffected by the thought of a needle in his arm. 'So are you and Dr Brodie sweethearts?' he asked cheekily. 'My auntie on Scuola says you make a lovely couple—I've heard her tell my mam!'

A posse of children around him burst into a fit of giggles and some of the parents remonstrated with them.

'Will you hush up, Jimmy?' scolded his mother. 'You're so rude. Do forgive him,' she pleaded. 'I'm afraid rumours get round this area very quickly…'

'It's quite all right, I'm immune to rumours,' said Terry, stretching her mouth into a false smile. 'There you are, Jimmy, you're all done now.' Beside her she was intensely aware that Atholl couldn't have helped but hear the exchange.

'I hope you've enjoyed your time in this area,' continued the woman politely.

'Yes,' sighed Terry. 'I have—very much.'

The last of the children had been seen and the hall was empty. Atholl started to push the chairs that had been used back against the wall and Terry wandered outside, unable to stand the atmosphere between the two of them in the empty room.

He came out into the sunshine and stopped for a second, taking in her woeful expression and the sad droop of her shoulders. Finishing their relationship evidently hadn't made her any happier, he thought.

'Right,' he remarked. 'Back to Scuola—and do I take it you're staying at the B and B tonight?'

'Yes. You can drop me off there.'

He nodded and got on the bike, and again there was the exquisite torture for her of being so close to Atholl as they flew along the road as she had been on the shores of the lake. Terry gave up trying to lean away from him as they drove along a winding road and allowed herself to squeeze up to his solid body, burying her head in the back of his leather jacket and savouring the warm, masculine smell of him. This would be the last time she would ever be this close to him, she cried inwardly to herself.

When they got off the boat the attractive house that did bed and breakfast was only a few minutes away. Atholl drew to a halt outside it and sat for a minute, waiting for Terry to dismount, then he got off the bike and took off his helmet, his dark hair ruffling in the breeze.

'I'll be ringing the agency for an emergency locum this afternoon,' he said tersely. 'Hopefully I can get one short term, starting in the next day or two.'

'Very well. I think it's for the best, Atholl.' Terry tried to sound calm and measured, to disguise the little catch in her voice. 'You'll let me know when one becomes available.'

She turned and went into the house and Atholl went back to The Sycamores and parked his bike against the wall as he was just going in to catch up on his e-mails. A young man smoking a cigarette and smartly dressed in a casual suede coat and cream cords was standing near the entrance, looking at the brass plaque on the wall that listed the doctors who worked there. Terry's name had not yet been added, so there were only Atholl and his uncle's names on it.

'Can I help you?' asked Atholl.

The man turned round and smiled. He was good looking in a tough kind of way, but with a hardness about him that reminded Atholl of the kind of youths he used to hang around with in Glasgow, although this man had a veneer of sophistication and polish about him.

'Thanks. I believe that Dr Younger works here—but I don't see her name on the plaque. I was hoping to meet up with her.'

'She has been working here,' answered Atholl brusquely. 'But she's leaving.'

'Ah...I see.' The man frowned slightly. 'And you are her colleague, I take it?'

'Yes, I am.' Atholl didn't elaborate—he felt tired and irritable and not willing to enter into a conversation with a stranger.

'You don't happen to know her address, do you? I seem to have mislaid it.'

Some instinct made Atholl wary of giving the man that information. 'I only know she's moved from the place she was living in very recently,' he said evasively. 'Are you a close friend?'

The young man smiled. 'Oh, yes, we were very close—and I knew her father very well.' He flicked his cigarette into the grass verge. 'Never mind, I'll catch up with her. As I said, she'll be expecting me.'

He walked off down the road and Atholl's gaze followed him. The first hint of anyone from Terry's background to have surfaced, he reflected as he went into the building, then his mobile phone rang and he answered it, putting the man out of his mind.

CHAPTER TEN

'I've got an emergency locum,' said Atholl tersely the next day, standing in front of the desk and looking down at Terry. 'He's starting tomorrow.'

So this is my last day here, and my successor is a man, Terry thought wryly. Not that she could blame Atholl—he'd surely never employ a woman again! She nodded wordlessly and sighed. The happiness she'd found in Scuola had been so short-lived. If only she could tell Atholl why she was leaving, what the whole background was. Impossible now. His safety depended on her cutting off any connection with him.

She bit her lip and said in a choked voice, 'Thanks for telling me, Atholl. I…I'm sorry it worked out like this.'

A moment's silence, then he said softly and unexpectedly, putting his hands on the desk and leaning towards her, deep blue eyes holding hers, 'So am I, Terry, so am I. You know it doesn't have to be like this. Are you quite, quite sure you want us to end things?' He looked at her searchingly. 'Is there something you're not telling me?'

She turned her face away from his, unable to meet his eyes, biting her lip. 'How do you mean?' Her voice was edgy, cautious.

Atholl shrugged and said simply, 'Because everything

seemed so right—you, me, the way we worked together. Sweetheart, I'm adding two and two together here and it's making five—there's no sense to it.'

His tender voice hung in the room so tantalisingly, just as he had sounded when he had made love to her that wonderful evening by the loch, and it was heart-breaking. Terry took a deep breath and got up from the desk, walking towards the window to get away from his scrutiny.

'It's for the best, believe me…'

He frowned and looked at her assessingly. She hadn't really answered his question. He stepped towards her and put out his hand to pull away a stray tendril of hair that covered her forehead, and she stiffened, willing him to move away again, to be anywhere but in that danger zone of closeness that made her stomach turn over. His hand strayed down her cheek and traced the line of her jaw down to her neck, and involuntarily she turned towards him, her face a picture of misery.

'Please, Atholl…don't…'

His hands were on the wall either side of her head, imprisoning her against it so that she couldn't escape, and his body was nearly against hers as he gazed at her with those clear blue eyes. He was too close—far too close for comfort!

'Tell me you don't love me, Terry,' he said roughly. 'Tell me now that we aren't meant to be together. It's not too late.'

His mouth came down and kissed her full on her lips, gently but possessively, his hands running lightly over the curving fullness of her breasts, turning her insides to liquid and reminding her of just what she would lose when they parted. And he was right—they should have been together, she thought in anguish. His touch became more demanding, his lips plundering hers, teasing them open, his body pressing urgently against her, and she felt her resolve sliding away, starting to respond helplessly to his passion.

Then Max's horrible note seemed to dance in front of her eyes and she forced herself to think of the danger she was putting Atholl in the longer she was near him. With every ounce of energy and resolve that she had, she twisted away from him and stood by the window, touching her lips where he had kissed them, still feeling them tingle.

'I can't get back with you, Atholl…I just can't,' she said desperately.

He straightened up and ran a hand roughly through his hair. 'I'm sorry, Terry.' He walked back to the desk, his back view slightly hunched as if gathering himself together, and after a few seconds turned round and said slowly, 'Very well, I shall have to accept it.' Then after a few seconds he added more briskly, 'By the way, some man was asking about you last night—said he was an old friend of yours and knew your father.'

A sudden chill of foreboding laid its fingers on Terry's heart. It had to be Max. There was no one else it could possibly be. So he'd got here already. Thank God she'd moved out of Atholl's cottage.

She swallowed and forced herself to say lightly, 'Really? Did you tell him my new address?'

'I'm not in the habit of giving private information to people I don't know.'

It was hard to hide the relief in her voice. 'No, of course not. Did he give his name?'

'No…I didn't have a chance to ask him. He was quite tall, fair haired—ring any bells?'

Terry shook her head. 'Can't think who it might be. Anyway, he'll probably find me if he needs to.' Her heart thumped uncomfortably, a picture of Max and those lazy hooded grey eyes smiling at her flashing into her imagination, and she shuddered. She forced herself to calm down and speak normally. 'I'll tidy up my desk, then, and update the notes for the new locum. I'll, er…see you before I go after tonight's surgery.'

'If you want to. I'll be here until I go to visit my uncle tonight.' Atholl turned round and went out of the room.

He walked slowly down the corridor to his surgery. Funny how she hadn't seemed excited that someone from London had come up to see her—someone who had known her father. But, then, Atholl mused, she never talked about her life in London or reminisced about her family. It was as if she had obliterated everything that had gone before her arrival in Scuola.

In the end Terry couldn't bear to say good bye to anyone. She knew how incredulous they would be that she was leaving when she had seemed to be so happy in her work. Instead, she left a note saying how much she had enjoyed her time with them, but unavoidable circumstances had meant she had to move on urgently, and that she would always remember Scuola and think of it fondly. She also left a short letter to Atholl.

The girls had all gone home, although she knew Atholl was still at the surgery because his bike was outside. She put the notes on the desk in the office and then after a wistful final look around the room she let herself out of the building and walked down to the bed and breakfast, looking around carefully to see no one was following her.

Atholl watched Terry walk down the street from his surgery window, until her slight figure neared the corner. Perhaps it was for the best that she hadn't come back to say goodbye personally. He sighed and was about to turn away when he noticed a man appearing from a side street and start to walk in the same direction. Nothing unusual in that, except that he recognised him as the man he'd spoken to last night who said he'd known Terry's father.

He watched as the man caught up with Terry. He must have said something to her because she stopped and turned round, then took a step back before the man took her arm. She seemed to be having a conversation with him and then, with the man still holding her arm firmly, they disappeared round the corner. She didn't look particularly surprised to see him.

Atholl wandered into the office, his mind preoccupied, slightly edgy. He saw two notes on the desk, one in Terry's writing addressed to him. He smiled bitterly as he picked it up and tore it open. It wouldn't be a love letter...

Atholl, please don't think badly of me. Believe me when I say I've never felt so happy as I did here with you. Meeting you was like coming alive again—a complete knockout to the heart. Perhaps I haven't put my reasons for leaving very clearly. I only know it's best that we part. I shall never ever forget you, Terry.

He frowned, fingering the note thoughtfully. She was saying that she hadn't been entirely clear about why she wanted to leave—was that a hint that there was more behind all this than she had told him? The uneasiness he had felt before flickered like a gathering fire through his mind. Something was not quite right about the whole thing. Intuitively he felt she was keeping something back from him.

A sudden wave of determination swept through him. Damn

it, he would go and see her at the bed and breakfast, whether that man was there or not, try and question her once and for all about this extraordinary decision of hers. He deserved a fuller explanation than she'd given him.

Mrs Bedowes, the woman who ran the bed and breakfast, answered the door.

'Dr Brodie!' she said in surprise. 'Can I help you?'

'I wondered if Dr Younger was here. I believe she's staying with you for a night or two?'

Mrs Bedowes shook her head. 'Well, no. She's just checked out, actually. She and her young man just came to collect her things—she's decided to leave tonight.'

Atholl raised an eyebrow. 'Her young man?'

'Oh, quite a charmer he was too. So much in love with her—he wouldn't let her out of his sight. He said he wished they'd had time to stay longer in such a lovely place as Scuola. Apparently Dr Younger has to do a quick home visit before they go off for a break, so she picked up her medical bag and case.'

'A home visit?' repeated Atholl, puzzled. As far as he knew, Terry had finished work and had no home visits planned.

'That's right,' said Mrs Bedowes with an indulgent smile. 'Her boyfriend wants to take her on a little holiday—they're such a sweet young couple. They were clinging to each other as if one of them might disappear!'

Terry's boyfriend? Atholl stared at the woman as a sudden extraordinary thought struck him. Was it possible that Max had come back into the picture? Was that why she'd finished things between them, because she'd realised she still loved the man, and knew he was coming to see her?

'Did…did you happen to catch this man's name?' he asked diffidently.

Mrs Bedowes smiled. 'Oh, yes, but only his first name. He answered his mobile in the middle of talking to me. I heard him say, "Max here."'

So that was it! Suddenly things were becoming clearer. Atholl stared at her wordlessly for a second, feeling as if someone had punched him in the solar plexus. Why the hell hadn't Terry told him the truth? Why keep it a secret that she was going back to Max, instead of reeling off all this garbage about not wanting to commit herself so soon after her affair with Max, and that things between himself and her had been going too fast?

She'd pretended that she hadn't a clue who Max was when Atholl had told her that a man had come to see her. But it had been a lie. She must have known damn well it had been Max but hadn't wanted Atholl to know.

A mixture of betrayal, rage and deep hurt flooded through him, but with a great effort he managed to control his voice, and said pleasantly enough, 'How long ago did they leave? I saw them going towards your place ten minutes ago.'

'Oh, they've only just gone.' The woman pointed up the road. 'They're in a blue car—they went up the main road towards the hills.'

'Thanks!' shouted Atholl over his shoulder, as he ran towards his motorbike and tried to kick-start it. It sputtered reluctantly into life and he roared off in the direction the woman had indicated. Again he felt slightly puzzled about Mrs Bedowes's reference to Terry going on a home visit. He tried to think of the patient she might be seeing on this route, thinking that at least it would give him a chance to catch up with her before she disappeared on this jaunt with a man she'd said had caused her great unhappiness.

What a fool he'd been! He should have realised that she was still hankering after that damn Max, but he had to confront her and hear from her own lips the whole truth this time. He was damned if he'd be fobbed off with a load of lies and half-truths.

If she was leaving because Max had come back into the picture, why hadn't she had the guts to tell him? Atholl felt a knot of anguish in his stomach—he'd thought more of Terry's honesty than that.

The bike was not performing well—he'd been meaning to strip it down and clean the plugs for some time. Every few minutes it seemed to die on him before surging back into life, and he decided that as he was passing his cottage, he'd stop there and take his car instead.

He was surprised to see that Shona was in the little garden when he arrived, barking her head off. He was sure he'd left the door closed when he'd gone to work. He got off his bike, propped it against the wall and bent down to ruffle Shona's fur.

'Have you seen Terry, old girl? And why are you outside?'

Shona wagged her tail furiously, then ran up and down the path, whining and looking back at Atholl. He looked around. No sign of anyone. It all looked very quiet, but Shona was obviously agitated. He followed the dog up the path and went up the step to open the door.

As soon as she felt that hand on her shoulder, Terry knew it was him—Max had caught up with her. She turned round slowly and looked into the distinctive pale grey eyes of the man she'd once thought she loved so much, and whom she'd last seen jumping into a car outside the bank on the day of the robbery. That was the day her father had been found bound and gagged in the office, the day he'd died of a heart attack.

Max had been wearing a balaclava and a tracksuit, but she'd known it was him all right—there was no disguising those unusual eyes of his and the old scar that cut across his eyebrow. She had recognised his accomplice in the get-away car—Max's brother, Harry, and he hadn't been wearing anything over his face. They'd screeched off round a corner and she had stood rooted to the spot, immobile with shock, shattered by the realisation that Max Carter was a criminal.

No one else had been in the road—it had been an early summer's evening and people had finished work and gone home. Terry had managed, with trembling fingers, to call for the police and, by some inner instinct, for an ambulance, then she'd gone and found her father tied up in his own office, obviously gravely ill. She'd tried desperately to massage her father's heart back to life, although she'd known that it had been too late—her beloved father had died.

In the months that had elapsed since that day, Max and Harry had gone to ground—completely vanished—and the police had said it was most likely they'd managed to flee the country, but they couldn't be sure. And now here was Max standing two feet away from her and looking at her with a familiar grin—good looking, charming even, but, as she now knew, an evil bastard.

'Hello, Theresa, surprised to see me?' he said. 'You didn't think I'd catch up with you so soon, did you? Thought changing your name and getting a new hairdo would be enough to keep you hidden?' He laughed softly. 'I'm not put off the scent that easily, you know.'

Cold terror gripped Terry's chest like a band forcing the

air out of her lungs, but she looked back at him steadily, her voice coming out strongly, scornfully, belying the fear she felt.

'I've nothing to say to you, Max, except this—you as good as murdered my father and you deserve to be in jail. I've informed the police about your horrible note.'

Max frowned, narrowing his eyes. 'You shouldn't have contacted the police, darling, not a clever thing to do. That note was between me and you, just to warn you that I need the money—when we've had our little talk.'

He took her arm and pulled her with him. 'I know where you're staying. I watched you take your cases to that B and B yesterday. Now you're going to come on a little holiday with me.'

Terry hung back, looking at him defiantly and telling herself what an insignificant-looking man he was. 'You can't make me. Anything you've got to say to me you can say it here and now!'

He came closer to her his lips a thin line. 'You know what I want. I need money to get away from here, start a new life.'

'I've no money on me...I can't arrange it so quickly,' Terry started to say.

He scowled. 'I told you to get some. I'll take you to a bank on the mainland and you can get some out—you doctors are well paid.'

By this time Max had pulled her round the corner and towards an old blue car just past the bed and breakfast place.

'And how will you make me do what you want, Max?' asked Terry coldly.

Max put his hand in his pocket and pulled out a handgun, at the same time pulling her towards him in what looked like an embrace to any passer-by. 'Perhaps this will persuade you, darling. Any nonsense and I won't hesitate to use it on you...or on anyone in our way.'

He meant it, thought Terry, her body shaking as she felt the muzzle of the gun press into her ribs. Max continued to hold her close to him.

'Before we do anything else I need some of your professional expertise, sweetheart. Harry's met with a little accident and I want your help in getting him right.'

'What's happened to him?'

'He got a bullet wound through his leg from an…acquaintance. The wound looks a bit black.'

Terry's mind raced—anything to buy time that might allow her to ring the police. 'I'll need to get my medical bag—it's at the B and B. We'll have to pick it up—I can't do anything without that.'

Max frowned. 'I thought you were a doctor—why do you need equipment?'

'If he's got any infection, he'll need antibiotics. There's penicillin in the bag…I may need tweezers to get the bullet out.'

Max pondered, biting his lip. 'OK,' he said at last. 'But you do what I say—we're lovers, understand?' Then with a cruel smile. 'Quite like old times, eh? Keep close to me and don't say anything you shouldn't.'

It took only a few minutes to get the medical bag and Terry's case. Mrs Bedowes, the owner of the B and B seemed unconcerned that Terry was checking out, and soon Max was pulling her back to his car, hugging her close to him. Harry was sitting in the back seat, lolling back and looking ashen, and a stain of blood had spread across his trouser leg. Terry was shoved in beside him and Max gave the gun to Harry.

'Keep that pointing towards her,' Max said. 'Don't worry, Harry, it's plain sailing so far. She'll fix up that leg of yours when we've got out of here.'

'It looks as if he's lost a lot of blood,' said Terry. 'I'll have to look at the wound pretty soon before he passes out.'

'Well, you're not looking at it in the village. We'll go into the hills first.'

Terry lay back in the car seat, her eyes closed. She knew it wasn't just money they wanted, or for her to look at Harry's wound—they needed to silence her for ever. She was, after all, the only witness who had seen the robbery, who knew for sure it was Max and Harry that had robbed the bank and caused her father's death.

The car stopped and she opened her eyes and saw that they'd parked the vehicle in a little copse before Atholl's cottage: it couldn't be seen from the road.

'Come on, darling, out you get.'

Terry was bewildered. 'Why have you stopped here?'

'For you to attend to Harry, of course. We know it's Dr Brodie's place, but I've been monitoring him. Tonight he's going to the mainland to see his uncle, and he won't be back for hours. Plenty of time for you to do the doctor bit for Harry and for us to have a coffee before we get going again.'

'I can't think why you're bothering with Harry—you didn't show such compassion for my father when you left him dying at the bank.'

Max grinned. 'Harry's my brother—the only person in the world I can trust.'

There were sounds of a car coming up the road behind them. Terry couldn't move her arms as they marched her along, but she threw back her head and screamed as loudly as she could. The car swept past, ignoring them.

Max pulled to a halt and turned Terry round towards him, drew back his hand and slapped her hard across the face, the signet ring he had on his little finger catching her cheek and slitting it open.

'Don't try that again. The next time it'll be more painful,' he snarled.

Terry sucked in her breath, her eyes stinging with tears at the pain, feeling blood oozing down her cheek. They pulled her up the path. Easy enough to kick the door open, and then throw her inside. Shona bounded towards her, barking delightedly and jumping up at her.

'Get that animal out of here,' growled Max to Harry. 'I don't like dogs.'

Harry gave Shona a casual kick out of the door and the dog yelped loudly, then turned round and snapped at the man's shoes. Another kick and poor Shona was out on the path and the door was slammed shut.

'How could you?' Terry screamed at Harry. 'What's the poor dog ever done to you?'

'Be quiet!' snapped Max. 'Sit down on that sofa.'

Terry sat down, trying to stop her limbs from trembling. She was damned if she'd show these men how terrified she was. At least they'd be gone by the time Atholl returned from seeing his uncle and he wouldn't be involved.

Then suddenly they heard the uneven sound of a motorbike coming up the road and stuttering to a halt in front of the cottage.

'Who the hell's that?' Harry turned a white, frightened face towards the door.

Max pulled Terry in front of him and held the gun against her head. 'Whoever it is, I won't give them the chance to get away.'

Terry looked in terror towards the door. She could hear Shona barking joyfully—it had to be Atholl returning early. Any minute he'd come in—and then what? They all waited, frozen, hardly breathing. A few minutes passed—still no sound except distant traffic coming up the road towards them.

'Where the hell is he?' muttered Harry uneasily. 'Perhaps he's taken the dog for a bleedin' walk.'

'Shut up!' snarled Max, tiptoeing to the window and peering out of the corner. 'He's not there. I think you're right, Harry, he's taken—'

There was a crash and the door from the kitchen burst open behind them. The men spun round and Atholl said, 'What the hell's going on?'

His gaze took in the scene of Terry with Max holding a gun to her head, and the prone body of Harry lying across the sofa with a large wound on his leg.

He sucked in his breath. 'Good God, Terry…' He turned to the two men and said in a low, harsh voice, 'What the hell have you done to Dr Younger?'

Max laughed unpleasantly. 'Dr Younger? You've been mis-informed, my friend. Allow me to introduce Dr Theresa Masterson.'

Atholl frowned and made to come towards Terry. 'I don't know what you're talking about, but put that bloody gun down.'

Max pressed his gun more firmly against Terry's head and said unsmilingly, 'Don't come any nearer, or else your colleague will get hurt. If you co-operate, we'll let her go, eventually.'

Atholl stood stock still, his blue eyes bright with fury, a muscle working in his cheek. 'You bastards…'

Max laughed, a coarse, cruel laugh. 'She knows a little too much about us, don't you, darling? We need to make a new life and we don't want her putting a spoke in our plans. A little money to help us get away would be a good start.'

'I see.' Atholl stepped back, looking at the men assessingly.

Then he said in a voice that was dangerously cool and unflurried, 'And how much were you thinking of?'

'We were thinking of ten thousand, but now you've appeared on the scene we might be tempted to take more…'

Terry watched Atholl with anguished eyes. He had been dragged into this and it had been her fault for not leaving the moment she'd known she'd been discovered. He looked so cool, so relaxed, as if there was nothing unusual about a gangster waving a gun in front of him.

Then several things happened at once. An explosion of sound. Both doors suddenly crashed open and several uniformed, shouting policemen burst into the room. Almost before they'd come in Atholl leapt at Max in the split second the man's attention had been diverted and punched him to the floor, forcing the gun out of his grip. Max lay there stunned for a minute, having hit his head hard on the fireplace surround, and was leapt on by one of the policemen. Harry was being held down on the floor between two policemen, his wrists handcuffed.

A large policeman helped to haul Atholl up from the floor where the force of the punch he'd given Max had landed him.

'We told you not to go in, Dr Brodie. You could have ruined the whole operation,' he growled. 'It was a risky thing to do…both of you could have been killed.'

Atholl looked slightly abashed. 'I couldn't wait,' he said simply. 'You weren't going to go in for ten minutes. God knows what could have happened in that time.'

'I'll be putting a report in,' grumbled the officer.

Atholl ignored the man and strode over to Terry, who was watching the scene with a mixture of bewilderment and relief. He sat on the sofa and put his arms round her. 'My darling, what's been going on?' he asked gently, touching her bruised and bleeding face delicately. 'Why didn't you tell me you were being threatened before? I was actually on my way to try and find you, and stopped off here to pick up my car. I was just about to open the door when a pack of policeman burst out of the bushes—apparently they've been shadowing you, hoping you'd lead them to these two brutes.'

Terry closed her eyes and big tears squeezed themselves out and rolled down her cheeks. 'I couldn't,' she whispered. 'I was told not to say anything about what happened in London. I'm so sorry, Atholl. I didn't think they'd find me here. I thought I was safe...and I didn't want you involved when—'

'It doesn't matter, it doesn't matter, sweetheart,' he murmured, cradling her head on his shoulder and rocking her backwards and forwards as one would a frightened child. 'All that matters is your safety. It's all behind you now.'

One of the policemen gave a polite cough. 'Excuse me, sir, we're taking these men away now. Er...perhaps when Dr Younger's had time to recover a little, you'd both come down to the station. I believe the Met will be sending up an officer to complete all the enquiries.'

As Max was led out he turned round to look at Terry. 'Didn't take long to find yourself someone new, did it, sweetheart?' he said bitterly.

The house seemed very quiet when all the policemen had gone, escorting Max and Harry to a police van. For several minutes Atholl remained holding Terry, neither of them speaking, then he turned her face toward him, bending his forehead to hers.

'And I thought you and that bloody man had got together

again, and that was the reason you'd finished things between us,' he said softly. 'That was why I came roaring after you, to make you tell me the truth, force you to admit that you still loved him.'

'How wrong you were,' said Terry wanly. She looked at Atholl with tears in her eyes. 'I couldn't tell you the truth because I loved you so much. I didn't want you to be involved. I'd been told it would be complete folly to reveal my background.'

Atholl took her hands in his. 'I can make an educated guess that you've been given a new identity—some sort of police witness protection?'

Terry nodded. 'It was all taken out of my hands really. Even the BMA was informed about my new name and the records changed. I was to get another job far from London through the agency you used. You see,' she added sadly, 'I thought Max really loved me. I was wrong. He wanted to get in with my father, gather information discreetly about the bank my father worked for, the times of cash deliveries—things like that.'

'Max seemed quite well spoken and educated—not the kind to want to rob a bank,' observed Atholl.

'He and his brother were gamblers—they needed plenty of money to pay their debts and fund their lifestyle.'

'But surely your father was very discreet about anything to do with the bank?'

'My father was quite a lonely man after Mum died. Over a few months he came to adore Max. They played golf together, Max took him racing, we all went to the theatre. Dad regarded him as the son he'd never had. Dad was thrilled I was going out with such a seemingly charismatic and successful man.'

Atholl nodded. 'He built up a rapport with your father, I'm sure, and your father would trust him.'

'Exactly. Max had led us to believe that he was a producer and a writer for a television company and my father was fascinated by the media world. After a while Max told him he had an idea for a play about—would you believe?—a gang of bank robbers. He asked my gullible father to help him write it. Of course, Dad was intensely flattered and excited—it gave him a new lease on life.'

'And after that I guess it was easy to extract information about bank practices regarding security, times of cash deliveries, and so,' said Atholl grimly.

Terry sighed. 'Dad was an innocent—and so was I, of course. Max manipulated my father so that he never realised he was being indiscreet.'

'But why were you on witness protection?' asked Atholl.

Terry took another long sip of her whisky, draining the glass, then said grimly, 'I was at the bank when the raid took place. I'd gone after work to meet my father, which I often did. We were going to have a meal out together. I waited by the side door I knew my father would use. I...I remember there was no one around, but a car with its engine running was parked at the other side of the street...'

Terry's voice faded a bit as the scene replayed itself in her mind.

'Go on,' prompted Atholl gently. 'Tell me everything.'

'Suddenly a man burst out of the door, almost knocking me over, and ran across the road to leap into the car. I knew instinctively it was a raid and rang the police on my mobile—and for some reason the ambulance as well.'

'And you knew who the man was?'

'Oh, yes.' Terry's voice was bitter. 'I could tell it was Max. His face was hidden, but he looked me right in the eyes—

there's no mistaking his eyes, they're a most unusual colour. I could easily see it was Harry, his brother, in the car—he wasn't covered up at all. Until that moment I had no idea that I'd been going out with a criminal—the man who caused my father's death.'

Atholl said quietly, 'Your father died—did they shoot him?'

'No,' said Terry in a small, sad voice. 'He'd been bound and gagged and he had a heart attack. I...I couldn't save him. I knew as soon as I saw him when I ran to his office that it was too late.'

Atholl hugged her to him, stroking her back comfortingly. 'A terrible, terrible thing...' he whispered. 'And I guess the police wanted you as a witness?'

'Without me, the police felt they didn't have enough evidence to secure a conviction even if they caught Max and Harry. I was told my life would be in danger if I stayed around while they were still at large.'

Atholl grinned. 'That's one thing you won't have to worry about now—those two won't be going anywhere in a hurry.'

Terry got up and wandered to the window, looking out at the beautiful view. She turned round and smiled brilliantly at Atholl. 'Yes, thank God. No more deception, no hiding the real story. At last I can be me again...Theresa Masterson. I'm a free woman!'

'I don't care what name you go under,' growled Atholl. 'When we made love underneath the stars that night on the shores of the loch, I knew that I'd found the woman I wanted to spend the rest of my life with. We've both had lucky escapes.'

Terry shook her head. 'I thought I'd never see you again,' she said. 'I thought you'd hate me for ending things so abruptly.'

'No, don't interrupt.' Atholl put his finger to Terry's lips for a second, gazing down into her eyes. 'When you said you wanted to end it between us it was the saddest day I can remember—but you know something? I didn't really believe you wanted to go—and I was right, wasn't I?'

He stroked a tendril of hair from her forehead, and Terry's heart began to do a little tattoo of happiness against her chest. She looked up at this man that she'd learned to love and thought she'd lost, and began to laugh.

'"Oh, what a tangled web we weave, when first we practise to deceive,"' she murmured, and looked up into his kind, wonderful face. 'If you really want me back, Atholl Brodie, that's all right with me!'

'I want more than that, Terry,' Atholl said with dancing eyes. 'I want you to change your name again—but for keeps this time. Don't you think Theresa Brodie sounds pretty good?'

EPILOGUE

SUNSHINE bathed the gardens of the Caledonian Hotel, and the little crowd of people on the terrace spilled down the steps and onto the lawn. Their happy chatter and clink of glasses drifted across the air and down to the shore of the sound, where the hotel had a little private dock with a small boat moored to it.

Atholl looked down at his dainty bride, sparkling in her long, fitted cream dress with its low-cut neckline and bodice covered with tiny seed pearls.

'You look so beautiful, Mrs Brodie,' he said huskily. 'I don't think I can wait to get this reception over and board the boat to go over the sea to our little bit of heaven on Skye…'

Terry looked up at impishly. 'You'll just have to contain yourself, darling. There's sixty people waiting to hang on your every word before we set off!'

Atholl groaned. 'Then I'll make the speech short for all our sakes!'

There can't be many moments in life that as are magical as this, thought Terry, looking across at the sun-kissed, sparkling sea and back to the guests surrounding her and Atholl. When she'd come on that first apprehensive day to Scuola she could never have imagined that a few months later she would be feeling this happy, her whole being bubbling with the euphoria of being loved by a man she adored. After the horror of Max, she'd given up on men, distrusting her own judgement, frightened of being betrayed again. And yet, against all the odds, she'd found just the man she needed.

'Are you not going to cut the cake yet, Atholl?' A tall woman with Atholl's blue eyes came up to them. 'Come on, son, we want to hear what you've got to say and then you can get off on that boat!'

'Don't worry, Mother. I'm as anxious to get off as you are to get rid of me!' Atholl grinned.

Mrs Brodie turned to her new daughter-in-law. 'And I'm very pleased that he chose the right lass—it took him long enough to find you,' she said softly, and her eyes twinkled. 'And it's about time I had some grandchildren!'

Cyril banged a gavel on the table holding the cake and said importantly, 'Ladies and gentlemen, pray silence for the groom, please!'

Atholl stood before the guests and pulled his bride towards him, looking down at her tenderly. 'Today, everyone, you see a man who couldn't be happier,' he said simply. 'I've met the love of my life, the most beautiful and marvellous woman in the world. I think I must have fallen in love with her the moment I first saw her on the quayside by the harbour the day she arrived. I know her parents would have been so proud of her, and I wish I could have met them to tell them that I will look after their darling daughter most carefully for the rest of my life!'

He raised his glass and smiled. 'To happiness,' he said. 'And to my precious Terry.' Then he kissed her gently.

Terry looked round at the assembled crowd and all the friends she'd made during her short time on Scuola—at

Isobel, outspoken, unsentimental, but still dabbing furiously at her eyes with a little hanky. Bunty and Sue were cheering loudly and Shona lay on the lawn, panting happily with a huge pink bow round her neck that Isobel had tied on. Even the two old Mackie sisters were there, sitting primly on chairs to listen to the speeches and sipping champagne rather cautiously.

'Help me step up onto the chair,' she whispered to Atholl, and then, once she was up, she smiled brilliantly at the guests, who fell quiet as they watched her.

'No need to tell you how happy I am,' she said. 'You on Scuola have become my family now, and I look forward to being part of your lives. I was very unhappy before I came here, but now...' She looked down at Atholl and smiled at him. 'Now I've found Atholl, everything's changed. It...it's like a dream come true!'

Then amidst the clapping there was the sudden skirl of pipes and a piper walked down the garden, playing a lilting tune. Atholl swung Terry down from the chair, and as people organised themselves to do an eightsome reel, he grabbed her hand.

'Come on, sweetheart, let's make a dash for it. Your case is on the boat so you can change later when we're out of sight!'

A few minutes later they were drawing away from Scuola across the sound, with the sun still dancing on the waves and the sky a rosy evening pink behind the hills. Atholl put his arm round Terry and pointed out to the water behind them.

'Looks like some other residents have come to wish us happiness,' he murmured.

A school of dolphins was leaping rhythmically out of the water, starting to follow the wake of the boat, their curving bodies silver in the sun.

'How perfect,' breathed Terry.

Her eyes filled with happy tears. How unexpectedly her life had turned around—from deep sadness to unbelievable happiness. A sudden cheer floated across the water from the guests as they realised that Terry and Atholl had left the party, and they both laughed and waved back to them.

'Dr and Mrs Brodie sail off on their new life,' whispered Atholl in her ear, hugging her to him.

A new life...the past forgotten, the future tantalising and exciting. And Terry knew that, whatever storms lay ahead, they could weather them together.

0609 Gen Std HB

JULY 2009 HARDBACK TITLES

ROMANCE

Marchese's Forgotten Bride	Michelle Reid
The Brazilian Millionaire's Love-Child	Anne Mather
Powerful Greek, Unworldly Wife	Sarah Morgan
The Virgin Secretary's Impossible Boss	Carole Mortimer
Kyriakis's Innocent Mistress	Diana Hamilton
Rich, Ruthless and Secretly Royal	Robyn Donald
Spanish Aristocrat, Forced Bride	India Grey
Kept for Her Baby	Kate Walker
The Costanzo Baby Secret	Catherine Spencer
The Mediterranean's Wife by Contract	Kathryn Ross
Claimed: Secret Royal Son	Marion Lennox
Expecting Miracle Twins	Barbara Hannay
A Trip with the Tycoon	Nicola Marsh
Invitation to the Boss's Ball	Fiona Harper
Keeping Her Baby's Secret	Raye Morgan
Memo: The Billionaire's Proposal	Melissa McClone
Secret Sheikh, Secret Baby	Carol Marinelli
The Playboy Doctor's Surprise Proposal	Anne Fraser

HISTORICAL

The Piratical Miss Ravenhurst	Louise Allen
His Forbidden Liaison	Joanna Maitland
An Innocent Debutante in Hanover Square	Anne Herries

MEDICAL™

Pregnant Midwife: Father Needed	Fiona McArthur
His Baby Bombshell	Jessica Matthews
Found: A Mother for His Son	Dianne Drake
Hired: GP and Wife	Judy Campbell

0609 Gen Std LP

MILLS & BOON®

Pure reading pleasure™

JULY 2009 LARGE PRINT TITLES

ROMANCE

Captive At The Sicilian Billionaire's Command	Penny Jordan
The Greek's Million-Dollar Baby Bargain	Julia James
Bedded for the Spaniard's Pleasure	Carole Mortimer
At the Argentinean Billionaire's Bidding	India Grey
Italian Groom, Princess Bride	Rebecca Winters
Falling for her Convenient Husband	Jessica Steele
Cinderella's Wedding Wish	Jessica Hart
The Rebel Heir's Bride	Patricia Thayer

HISTORICAL

The Rake's Defiant Mistress	Mary Brendan
The Viscount Claims His Bride	Bronwyn Scott
The Major and the Country Miss	Dorothy Elbury

MEDICAL™

The Greek Doctor's New-Year Baby	Kate Hardy
The Heart Surgeon's Secret Child	Meredith Webber
The Midwife's Little Miracle	Fiona McArthur
The Single Dad's New-Year Bride	Amy Andrews
The Wife He's Been Waiting For	Dianne Drake
Posh Doc Claims His Bride	Anne Fraser

0709 Gen Std HB

MILLS & BOON

ROMANCE

Desert Prince, Bride of Innocence	Lynne Graham
Raffaele: Taming His Tempestuous Virgin	Sandra Marton
The Italian Billionaire's Secretary Mistress	Sharon Kendrick
Bride, Bought and Paid For	Helen Bianchin
Hired for the Boss's Bedroom	Cathy Williams
The Christmas Love-Child	Jennie Lucas
Mistress to the Merciless Millionaire	Abby Green
Italian Boss, Proud Miss Prim	Susan Stephens
Proud Revenge, Passionate Wedlock	Janette Kenny
The Buenos Aires Marriage Deal	Maggie Cox
Betrothed: To the People's Prince	Marion Lennox
The Bridesmaid's Baby	Barbara Hannay
The Greek's Long-Lost Son	Rebecca Winters
His Housekeeper Bride	Melissa James
A Princess for Christmas	Shirley Jump
The Frenchman's Plain-Jane Project	Myrna Mackenzie
Italian Doctor, Dream Proposal	Margaret McDonagh
Marriage Reunited: Baby on the Way	Sharon Archer

HISTORICAL

The Brigadier's Daughter	Catherine March
The Wicked Baron	Sarah Mallory
His Runaway Maiden	June Francis

MEDICAL™

Wanted: A Father for her Twins	Emily Forbes
Bride on the Children's Ward	Lucy Clark
The Rebel of Penhally Bay	Caroline Anderson
Marrying the Playboy Doctor	Laura Iding

MILLS & BOON

AUGUST 2009 LARGE PRINT TITLES

ROMANCE

The Spanish Billionaire's Pregnant Wife	Lynne Graham
The Italian's Ruthless Marriage Command	Helen Bianchin
The Brunelli Baby Bargain	Kim Lawrence
The French Tycoon's Pregnant Mistress	Abby Green
Diamond in the Rough	Diana Palmer
Secret Baby, Surprise Parents	Liz Fielding
The Rebel King	Melissa James
Nine-to-Five Bride	Jennie Adams

HISTORICAL

The Disgraceful Mr Ravenhurst	Louise Allen
The Duke's Cinderella Bride	Carole Mortimer
Impoverished Miss, Convenient Wife	Michelle Styles

MEDICAL™

Children's Doctor, Society Bride	Joanna Neil
The Heart Surgeon's Baby Surprise	Meredith Webber
A Wife for the Baby Doctor	Josie Metcalfe
The Royal Doctor's Bride	Jessica Matthews
Outback Doctor, English Bride	Leah Martyn
Surgeon Boss, Surprise Dad	Janice Lynn